PRAISE FOR
THE TEMPTAION SAGA

"Is it hot in here? Congratulations, Ms. Hardt. You dropped me into the middle of a scorching hot story and let me burn."
~ Seriously Reviewed

"I took this book to bed with me and I didn't sleep until 4 a.m. Yes, it's that damn engrossing, so grab your copy now!"
~Whirlwind Books

"Temptation never tasted so sweet... Both tempting, and a treasure... this book held many of the seductive vices I've come to expect from Ms. Hardt's work."
~Bare Naked Words

Trusting
SYDNEY

THE TEMPTATION SAGA
BOOK SIX

WATERHOUSE PRESS

Trusting

SYDNEY

THE TEMPTATION SAGA
BOOK SIX

In memory of the real Sydney and Sam

PROLOGUE

Denver, Colorado, Five Years Earlier

"Hey, Sam...Chad."

Sam O'Donovan looked up. His sister was on the arm of Zach McCray.

"Hey, Dust." He turned to his companions. "This is my baby sister, Dusty. Dusty, meet Sydney Buchanan and Linda Rhine."

"And this is my big brother Zach," Chad said. "You all want to sit down?"

"We'd love to," Dusty said.

"Sydney's a barrel racer," Sam said. "I've been telling her all about you."

"Are you competing?" Dusty asked.

"Yeah. Day after tomorrow. You?"

"Day after tomorrow. Good luck to you."

"You too. Though I doubt you'll need it. Sam told me about your best time. Thirteen point nine seconds is awesome."

"Sydney's real good too," Sam said. "Her personal best is fourteen point one."

"That's exceptional," Dusty said. "I see you'll be some real competition."

"You want to dance, darlin'?" Zach asked Dusty. "They're firing up the music."

"Sure."

She and Zach left the table, and Sam focused his gaze on

the black-haired beauty next to him. Sydney Buchanan's dark eyes mesmerized him. He'd never been one to pick up a girl he hardly knew, but his old friend Chad was obviously a pro at it. He was charming the pants off Miss Linda Rhine this very minute in the Westminster Room at the Windsor Hotel. The Bay siblings did know how to throw a party.

Course, they had money to burn.

Chad took the last swill of his beer and set the empty bottle on the table. "You all want to get on outta here? Go for dinner somewhere?"

"Sounds great to me," Linda said, shaking her blond curls.

Sam turned to Sydney. "How about it?"

She blinked slowly. "Sure, I suppose it's okay."

Damn, those eyes could hypnotize a grizzly.

"Great." Chad stood. "I know a fantastic little Italian place not too far from here. They always have a table for me."

They walked through the room. Zach and Dusty were sitting at a table, eating appetizers from the huge spread.

"We're heading out," Chad said to them. "We're going for a late supper at Amici's. You all want to come?"

Zach shook his head. "No thanks. We have plans."

"Okay, see you guys later." Sam followed Chad, who was already very cozy with his arm around Linda, out the door of the ballroom.

His own hand itched to touch beautiful Sydney. Her dark hair fell to her bottom. The nearly onyx waves glided as she walked, keeping time with her pace. She walked slightly ahead of Sam, and his gaze never left her. Should he touch her?

How I want to touch her.

He wasn't a ladies' man like Chad. He'd had experience, of course, but getting too friendly on a first date—and this wasn't even a first date—wasn't his style. They'd just met at the Bays' party. Getting too friendly on a first *meeting* was definitely not his style. He prided himself on being a gentleman.

Besides, he hadn't had much time for dating during the past several years. First Dusty's illness, and then their father's death, and then nearly losing the farm—not too many moments left for wooing the ladies.

He was totally out of practice. Hopefully he wouldn't make a complete ass of himself.

Chad was right. Amici's had a great table for them, private and out of the way, with a beautiful view of downtown Denver in lights.

His baked ziti was delicious. He didn't say much, just watched Sydney eat her pasta—how could one woman be so sexy eating pasta?—while Chad and Linda rattled on about one thing and another.

"What about you, Syd?" Linda said.

Sam jerked toward the female voice. She was asking Sydney something, but damned if he knew what. He hadn't been listening.

"I've got a fair shot, I guess," Sydney replied. "But Sam's sister is going to be tough to beat."

Okay. They're talking about the barrel racing. Sam nodded. "Dusty's good, that's for sure."

"Why haven't you all been down here to nationals before?" Chad asked.

Sam hesitated. He didn't like talking about their financial situation, especially not to one of the McCray heirs. Chad could write his own ticket anywhere.

"Just haven't had the time, I guess."

Chad pushed his empty plate away from him. "I don't

know about the rest of you, but I'm stuffed."

"Couldn't eat another bite." Linda winked.

They've got somethin' up their sleeves.

"We could go back to my suite," Chad said. "Have a few drinks."

Yep, I know what he has in mind. And three—or four—is a crowd. Sydney's gaze locked onto his, her dark eyes brooding.

Damn!

He couldn't take her back to his room at the Holiday Inn. Not only was it not up to the Windsor Hotel standards, but he shared it with Dusty. Not exactly fare for a romantic evening.

"I don't know," he said. "I've got lots to do tomorrow, and it's getting late."

"Don't be a party pooper, Sam." Chad guffawed. "The girls are stayin' at the Windsor. Let's go on back there. The night's still young."

Sydney reached toward him, and her small hand landed on his forearm. His groin tightened.

She blinked those dark eyes slowly and her lips curved into a shy smile.

"We could go to my room."

CHAPTER ONE

Bakersville, Colorado, Present Day

"Ladies and gentlemen," Mark, the rodeo emcee announced. "Welcome to the opening ceremonies of the Bakersville Rodeo! We've got a week full of fun and adventure planned for everyone. Zach and Dusty McCray have brought back their bull, El Diablo, and they're still offering that half-mil purse to anyone who can ride him for a full eight seconds. Maybe this is the year. Any of you cowboys up for the challenge?

"Our rodeo queen contest is underway, and we'll have this year's pretty ladies come out and strut their stuff in a minute. First, though, please welcome last year's rodeo queen, Amber Cross. Miss Cross is escorted by her father, the one and only Thunder Morgan!"

Sam stood in the McCray brothers' private box at the rodeo arena, taking care of his nephew, Sean. Deafening applause echoed from the stands. A platinum blond siren took the stage on his idol's arm.

Thunder Morgan. The best bronc buster in history, in Sam's humble opinion. He hadn't always won, but he'd always given the audience a good show. The man had style. Too bad he'd retired a few years back.

"Amber won't be single much longer. Next week, after she crowns our new rodeo queen, she'll become Mrs. Harper Bay!"

More thundering applause.

"Congratulations, Amber," Mark said.

"Thank you so much, Mark. I've enjoyed being your queen for a year, but I'm going to love being Mrs. Bay for the rest of my life."

"Well said, Amber. Mr. Morgan, it's an honor to have you here at our small-town rodeo. But I understand you've been here before."

"Yup," Thunder said. "Busted broncs here fifteen years ago and won a large purse. Thank you, Bakersville!"

Thundering applause again. Amber and her father left the stage as Mark introduced the grand marshal of this year's parade, Sam's brother-in-law, Zach McCray.

Sam stopped listening as Mark and Zach traded jibes. Zach was a good man. He took amazing care of Dusty and their son, Sean. Sam could never repay him for that, and the beauty was that Zach didn't expect repayment. He adored his wife and son.

"Hey, Sam, look who I found."

Zach turned to see his sister and a gorgeous black-haired beauty enter the box.

He gulped.

"You remember Sydney, don't you?"

Sydney Buchanan.

She hadn't changed one bit in five years, except maybe she was more beautiful.

"Of course," he said. "Hello." He held out his hand.

When she took it, sparks sizzled up his arm. Those brooding dark eyes seared into his own.

"It's wonderful to see you again, Sam."

"Isn't this great?" Dusty took Sean's hand. "Thanks for watching him."

"No problem. You know I love the little guy."

"He's adorable." Sydney squatted down. "How old are you, sweetie?"

"I'm almost five," Sean said.

"You're almost a grown-up." Sydney touched the little boy's cheek and stood. "You must feel incredibly lucky."

Dusty smiled. "Only every minute of every day."

Was that a hint of sadness in Sydney's dark eyes? Sam wasn't sure. Did she know about Dusty's cancer, and that little Sean was almost a miracle? It wasn't common knowledge outside Bakersville. At least he didn't think it was.

"Are you competing this year, Sydney?" Dusty asked.

"Sure am. That's why we're here. Are you?"

Dusty shook her head. "Nope. I haven't competed since that ill-fated race against you back in Denver all those years ago. I ended up pregnant with Sean and never went back to racing."

"You gave it all up? Even bull riding?"

Dusty laughed. "*Especially* bull riding. Zach wouldn't hear of it, and I actually agreed with him. We were lucky to get Sean. It's unlikely I'll ever get pregnant again."

"Oh." Sydney looked down. "I'm sorry. I didn't mean to bring up anything...well, you know."

So she wasn't aware of the situation. Then why did she look so sad?

"I know you didn't." Dusty smiled again. "It's okay."

Sam truly admired his baby sister. She was the strongest woman he knew. She'd been to hell and back, yet a genuine smile always graced her pretty face.

"You should have won that race, anyway," Sydney said. "You were magnificent."

Dusty let out a sigh and pulled Sean into her arms. "Things

worked out for the best, believe me. Look what I got for my trouble. I'm a lucky woman."

Sydney's red lips curved into a half smile. "Yes, you sure are."

"Sam, I've invited Syd and her family to the house tonight for our little get-together."

Sam's heart lurched. Was he happy or unhappy at the news? What exactly did one say to a woman he'd slept with once and never seen again?

The sex had been good. Freaking amazing, actually. None of his other experiences had come close. He shuddered as the image of her crimson lips wrapped around his cock sprang into his mind. She'd licked and teased him until he thought he'd burst.

He dismissed the thought. *Don't need a boner right now.*

Two days later, Sydney had won the barrel race with a time of 14.9 seconds—not a personal best, but damn good.

But her victory had been bittersweet for Sam. Dusty and her mare had out-performed Sydney until the last second, when they knocked over the third barrel. The five second penalty had cost Dusty the race.

Her last race.

Course as she'd said, things had worked out. She married Zach McCray a few months later and had Sean not long after.

"Sam's psyched," Dusty continued, "because Thunder Morgan will be there. He's the father of one of my sister-in-law's best friends."

Great. Now he looked like a star struck little boy to Sydney.

"Really? That's awesome," Sydney said.

"He's been Sam's idol for years."

Shut up, Dusty!

"Do you still bust broncs, Sam?" Sydney asked.

"Yep. I've got a couple competitions this week. I'm thinking about giving El Diablo a try too."

Dusty's eyebrows shot up. "What?"

"You heard me."

"Wow! I remember that bull," Sydney said. "I didn't know you rode bulls, Sam."

"He doesn't," Dusty said.

"I've ridden a few in my day."

"You don't know Diablo."

"You rode him, didn't you?"

"And damn near killed myself and Zach too, if you recall." Dusty put Sean down. "Go play with your Legos, sweetheart."

Sam berated himself silently. He had no intention of riding that bull. He'd only said it to impress Sydney. At thirty-three, he didn't need to be talking himself up to impress some babe. High school had been a long time ago, for God's sake, yet here he was talking big for a girl.

"You two are both amazing," Sydney said. "I'd never get on a bull."

"You just have to understand them, " Dusty said. "They're really sweet, beautiful animals."

"No offense, but every time I watch bull riding, I think those guys are insane."

Dusty laughed. "Some of them are, that's for sure. I know the whole town thought I was when I got on Diablo."

Sam opened his mouth to agree but shut it quickly. Since he'd opened his trap to say he might ride the damn bull, he couldn't very well agree that his sister had been crazy to attempt it.

And no doubt, she *had* been crazy.

Dusty was actually really good with bulls, with all animals. She had originally planned to study veterinary medicine, but her illness, and then her marriage and birth of her son, had changed that goal long ago. Still, she helped her sister-in-law Annie, who was the town vet, as often as she could.

"You guys are still offering that half-mil purse, huh? No one's won it yet?"

"Not yet," Dusty said. "We have a couple cowpokes try every year. Thankfully no one's been seriously hurt."

"Do you still work with him?"

"I take care of him. I haven't tried to ride him again. Like I said, I gave all that up when I got pregnant."

"Yeah, I understand." Sydney's gaze shot to Sean, who was sitting on the floor with his Legos. "Your little boy is beautiful."

"Thank you. We think so."

"So what time are you starting tonight?" Sydney fidgeted a little and played with her hair.

Did she not want to go to Dusty's shindig? Why on earth not? His baby sister and her hubby threw a party like nobody's business.

"Around six. Come on over any time. We'll have a dinner buffet, but it's a 'serve yourself and eat when you want to' kind of thing."

Sam laughed. "Don't listen to her. The McCrays don't do anything halfway. Their 'serve yourself' buffet will be an open bar and a huge spread topped with a baron of McCray beef."

Sydney blinked again. Clearly, the woman was a bit nervous. Because of him? Couldn't be. Five years had passed since their clandestine liaison. No reason to be nervous.

Course his own belly was doing a series of somersaults.

He excused himself and left the box. He found an empty seat in the rafters and plunked down.

Sydney Buchanan.

She hadn't changed a bit. In fact, if it were possible, she looked even sexier and more beautiful.

They had shared an amazing night all those years ago, still the most passionate night he'd ever spent. Bits and pieces of their crazy lovemaking still haunted him regularly, but a long time had passed since he'd relived the entire night.

Opening ceremonies were still going on, but soon Mark's voice became unintelligible, and a vision appeared in Sam's mind.

★ ★ ★

"We could go to my room."

How had they gotten there? Sam wasn't sure, but sure as day, here he was in Sydney Buchanan's hotel room, kissing those beautiful red lips.

He stiffened as she sighed softly into his mouth. He traced his tongue around her luscious full lips and gently eased it into her sweet mouth.

The soft sigh again—it vibrated sweetly against his inner cheeks. He deepened the kiss.

Her response was immediate. Her soft tongue swept against his own. A girl who liked tongue as much as he did. Heaven on Earth. The kiss became more frantic, more urgent. Their tongues tangled together, and Sydney's soft sighs turned into low moans.

She pressed her full breasts against his chest. More heaven. Sam couldn't remember a time when he'd desired a woman this much. He urged her forward until they hit the wall next to the bathroom. He pushed her against the hard surface and ground his erection against her. He was so hard he thought he might burst.

Still they kissed, fully clothed, moaning into each other's mouths. When she ripped away from him and inhaled, he rained wet kisses over her cheek and her neck, spurred by the frantic need that welled within him.

Her scent intoxicated him. Green apples or pears, fruity and inebriating, mixed with a feminine musk all her own. A deep hunger swelled in his groin, and his thoughts strayed to her hidden core. Would she be wet for him? Would she taste as good as she smelled?

He'd soon find out.

But first, the silky skin of her shoulders and the plump swell of her breasts beckoned him.

A few whispered words escaped her lips in a soft breathy caress against his neck. What had she said? He wasn't sure, but they were a husky sound, a helpless sound. A sound of want and desire.

"Do you want me, Sydney?"

"God, yes."

She wore a little black dress—sexy and classic—and right now he couldn't wait to get it off her.

He slid one spaghetti strap off her milky shoulder and pressed his lips to the smooth skin. Fire blazed through his veins. He inhaled, drinking in her fruity, musky fragrance.

She sighed. "That feels so good."

"Good, honey. I want to make you feel good. I want to take you to the stars."

He moved to the other strap and eased it over her creamy

flesh. This time he kept going, until he exposed her rosy bosom.

"My God, you're beautiful." He cupped both breasts.

"Yes. Touch me. Please."

A chuckle left his throat. "Since you asked so nicely."

He thumbed both nipples until they were hard and erect beneath his fingers. He tugged at them until he could resist no longer. Then he lowered his mouth to one peak and licked it lightly.

"Yes," she said again. "Yes, suck my nipple."

A girl who liked to talk during sex. Another plus. He clamped his lips over the hard bud. Her texture was satin against his tongue and oh so sweet. He'd never come across nipples that had a flavor before. Or maybe he just wanted this woman like he'd never wanted another.

Crazy. They'd just met. He wasn't one to screw on the first date—if this was even a date. But damned if it didn't feel like the rightest thing he'd done in years.

She sure wasn't complaining either. To be on the safe side, he lifted his mouth from her nipple and met her dark gaze. "You sure about this, sweetheart?"

She nodded, and her smile lit her face like the lights on a country Christmas tree. "I'm very sure. I want you, Sam."

His cock roared to life. "I want you too. God, I want you."

He lowered his head and took the other nipple between his lips. He licked and nibbled, enjoying her moans as she writhed against him. He slid the dress down her side, over the hills of her hips, over her thighs, until it lay crumpled on the floor in a black puddle. He eased her panties down and she stepped out of them. A triangle of black pointed the way to ecstasy. He reached between her legs and smoothed his fingers through her folds. Slick. Moist. Wet.

So wet.

He groaned. "Wet, sweetheart."

"For you," she said, her voice a breathy whisper.

His erection strained harder against the confines of his black pants. They were a loose fit, but damned if they weren't tight as a bowstring right now.

"Take me to bed, Sam."

No need to ask twice. Naked except for her strappy silver sandals, she stood, ruby lips parted, dark hair cascading over silk skin, looking like a creamy dessert.

Still fully clothed, he lifted her in his arms and carried her to the bed. He laid her on the cool sheets, sat down, and started unbuttoning his shirt.

She sat up. "Let me," she said and took over undressing him. With each button and newly exposed skin, she kissed him.

And with each kiss, his skin tightened, and blood rushed through his veins and settled in his already throbbing erection. He felt her kisses in every pore of his body, every pulse of his heart. Heat curled inside him, threatening his control.

When his shirt lay in a heap on the floor, she started on his pants. A drop of fluid darkened a hole-punch-size spot on his boxer briefs. She smiled, and he knew she had noticed.

He didn't care. It was no secret how much he wanted her. His rock-hard cock was evidence enough of that.

She eased the boxers and pants over his legs, and her eyes widened.

"You're so muscular. God, your legs are amazing."

He smiled. "Thank you."

"But this"—she slid her hands up his thighs to his cock—"is truly a work of art." She kissed the head lightly, licking away another drop of fluid.

He jerked. Just one tiny touch from her lips on his cock and he was ready to explode. "God, sweetheart. Damn, that feels good."

"Mmm, then this'll feel even better." She took his length between her lips.

Sweet God in heaven! He couldn't come yet. Had to get inside her. But oh, how her mouth tantalized him. On top of the incredible feeling, the image of her full lips gliding over his cock was a major turn-on.

And he hadn't thought it possible to get more turned on.

Oral sex was good no matter what, but Sydney Buchanan had elevated it to a fine art. She alternated swirling her tongue around the head and thrusting her mouth up and down his length. Every time he thought he'd burst, she eased up and brought him back down.

Good thing, too, because this night wasn't ending before he tasted the treasure between those long, beautiful legs.

Gently he grabbed both her cheeks and pulled her toward him for a long, deep kiss. His own saltiness on her tongue drove him crazy, but before he got too frantic, he turned her over so she lay on her back. He broke the kiss and spread her lovely legs.

Between them, her glistening sex beckoned. He kissed each nipple, trailed his lips down her smooth belly to her vulva, and then to her moist folds.

Like silk beneath his tongue. She tasted of sweet pear, of morning dew. He flicked her hard clit with his tongue and then buried it in her wet channel.

She writhed beneath him. "Yes, just like that. Please."

He continued, adding one finger, and then another, all the while licking her, until she clamped down on his hand.

"Yes! I'm coming."

She didn't have to say it. He knew by the pulsing within her against his fingers and tongue.

And God, he was thrilled.

He had to have her, and he had to have her now.

He gently eased his fingers from her and left the bed for a moment to grab his wallet out of his pants and the condom out of his wallet. He sheathed himself in record time and plowed into her tight depths.

"God!" So good, so very good. He pumped and pumped, her hips rising to meet him. He met her mouth with a sizzling kiss, all the while thrusting harder and faster.

When he'd almost reached the brink, he pulled out, turned her over gently, and entered her from behind.

Doggy style. He loved that position. Loved them all. He wanted her on top next, riding him like she rode her barrel racing mare. Only faster and stronger and never ending.

He thrust again. Her sweet ass cheeks wiggled against his hips—beautiful. Everything about her was beautiful, but Sam was a self-professed ass man.

Well, and a boob man.

Aw, hell, he loved it all.

Even her back was sexy—smooth and creamy and all her.

Sydney.

What a woman.

Finally, he could hold out no longer.

"Now, honey, now," he said, and he reached underneath her and rubbed her swollen clit.

When her orgasm began, he let go. Tiny convulsions started at the base of his cock and spread through his length. As the orgasm erupted, the spasms darted through his body, spreading to his arms and legs. Nirvana. He went rigid and plunged into *her as far as he could, letting the climax take him.*

Shudders racked his body, and when the contractions finally died down, his legs shook. When he stood to dispose of the condom, they felt like jelly.

They rested a bit, shared a glass of wine.

Then they started again.

★ ★ ★

Sam saw only darkness. He opened his eyes. When had he closed them? His erection pressed against his jeans. Well, wouldn't be getting up from this seat for a while. Good thing the opening ceremonies were still going on. Man, that Mark guy was a windbag. Was it really necessary to introduce the florist? Sheesh.

The memory of that night filled Sam with happiness.

Happiness. How long had happiness been missing from his life?

He wasn't *un*happy. Not at all. Yet life had grown stale. He simply existed from day to day. Even when he went on the road to rodeos, as now, his life held little meaning. No one needed him anymore. Dusty had Zach and their son. His ranch was thriving and his able foreman took care of everything. He had dated a few times in the last several years, but he hadn't found anyone who really brought meaning into his life.

Day to day to day to day—the life of Sam O'Donovan.

But at this moment, he was smiling. Joy coursed through his veins.

Sydney Buchanan.

He'd tried once to look her up after he returned to Montana but hadn't kept looking for very long. He'd had a bankrupt ranch to look after. He could have found her if he'd looked harder.

He'd given up.

No more giving up.

He motioned to a vendor selling beer. Too bad they didn't sell shots of bourbon. He could use a stiff one—to help him get rid of his other stiff one.

Sydney Buchanan.

She'd be at Dusty's party tonight.

And she'd be in Sam's bed come morning.

CHAPTER TWO

"Sammy, it's great to have you back in town!" Chad McCray slapped Sam on the back. "I don't get to see my only blood brother enough."

Sam laughed, though the comment saddened him. He and Chad had become blood brothers the day Sam and his family had left McCray Landing where his father worked as a ranch hand. They went back to Montana to stay with his mother's family when she was dying of leukemia.

Though the disease had taken his mother, it had spared his baby sister, thank God. Dusty had responded well to treatment and was now considered cured. She was the picture of health and country-girl beauty, roaming around the crowd and playing hostess in her red gingham blouse and denim miniskirt.

Chad excused himself, and Sam turned to see Dusty approach an older gentleman. Sam jerked in his boots. *Thunder Morgan*. Dusty grabbed the man's arm and pulled him toward Sam. The rodeo queen and her boyfriend trailed behind.

"Sam," Dusty said, "I know this is someone you've been dying to meet."

Sam stuck out his hand. "Mr. Morgan, it's an honor."

The man chuckled. "It's Thunder or Morgan, take your pick. But never Mr. Morgan. Nice to meet you." He turned toward the other two. "Have you met my daughter, Amber, and her fiancé, Harper Bay?"

Sam nodded. "I know Harper. How are you?"

"Good, good," Harper said.

"And Amber, it's a pleasure. You are one beautiful rodeo queen."

Amber's delicate skin turned rosy, and she shook her platinum waves. "Thank you. It's nice to meet you. Dusty raves about you. We're so glad you'll be able to stay in town for our wedding next week."

"I wouldn't miss it," Sam said.

"I know you have lots of questions for Thunder," Dusty said.

Sam nodded. He did. A million, maybe. But at the moment, his tongue was tied in a knot.

Clad in denim shorts and a white camisole, her dark gaze scanning the party, was none other than Sydney Buchanan.

"Sydney!" Dusty motioned her toward them.

She walked toward them slowly. With a little trepidation maybe? Sam wasn't sure.

"Where are your parents?" Dusty asked.

"They decided to stay at the hotel," Sydney said. "My little brother isn't feeling well tonight."

Little brother? Sam knew Sydney had an older brother, Blake, who lived in Bakersville now. But a younger one? Still a lot he didn't know about this gorgeous woman.

"I'm sorry to hear that," Dusty said. "I really wanted him and Sean to meet. They're almost the same age."

Sydney smiled, her lips trembling ever so slightly. Was she nervous?

"Some other time. I'm sure they'll hit it off."

Dusty made the necessary introductions, and Thunder, Amber, and Harper excused themselves to get a drink.

"That sounds like a good idea," Sam said. "Would you like a drink?"

Sydney shook her head and cleared her throat. "On second thought, yes."

"What'll it be? It's full bar here, like I told you."

She smiled. "How about a dry martini?"

"Sounds great." He walked her over to the bar.

"A dry martini for the lady, and a Fat Tire for me." Sam shoved a few dollar bills into the bartender's tip jar and handed the martini to Sydney.

"Thank you," she said shyly.

Was this a coy routine? She sure hadn't been shy that night five years ago. In fact, *she* had invited him to her room, not the other way around.

Course five years was a long time. People did change. Who knew what had happened to her in half a decade? No matter. Sam planned to learn all he could about Miss Sydney Buchanan this evening.

But before he could ask the first question, she excused herself to make a phone call.

Damn.

★ ★ ★

Calm down, Syd. Jesus.

She'd handled this much better at the rodeo. Still, her heart had thumped so hard against her sternum she'd thought for sure Sam could see it.

Now, in this slinky camisole—which had been a mistake, by the way—it must be completely obvious. She leaned against the counter in the downstairs bathroom and regarded her image in the mirror. What had she been thinking?

He was as handsome as she remembered—sandy brown hair, expressive brown eyes, and that body! He'd been ripped head to toe five years ago, and from what she could see, that hadn't changed. If anything, he looked even better. His dark jeans hugged those slim hips and that perfect butt just right—not too tight, but tight enough to see the gorgeous musculature.

She hadn't seen him bust broncs. She hadn't seen him at all after that one night, even though they'd both been in Denver at the Stock Show for the next few days. He hadn't tried to contact her.

A veil of guilt blanketed her. Nor had she tried to contact him.

She should have called.

Yes, *he* could have called. But she *should* have.

No matter. They were just two ships that had passed during one amazing night. They could never pass again for myriad reasons, none of which she could dwell on at the moment.

Why had she come to this party? She'd known it was a bad idea. Dusty McCray was such a sweetie to invite her. Sydney was amazed Dusty had remembered her after so long.

I suppose you never forget your final barrel race.

Sydney hadn't forgotten that race either. She'd won a sizable purse, and it had been her last race for about a year and a half.

She'd been back for a couple years now. She had done well but hadn't been overly successful. Hopefully this rodeo would be good to her. She needed to win a purse—a big one.

She made a quick phone call to her parents at the hotel to check on Duke, and then took a deep breath and left the security of the bathroom. She could make excuses to Dusty easily enough. She wasn't feeling well, or she had to get up early to work her mare tomorrow, or any number of other things could get her out of this house, away from Sam O'Donovan.

In fact, she was tempted to just leave quietly, but that would be rude. Dusty had been so nice to her, and Sydney was not a rude person. She couldn't just leave.

She inhaled again and let out the air slowly. Find Dusty and get the heck out of Dodge.

Finding Dusty meant going out back again, and going out back again meant the risk of running into Sam. It was a chance she'd have to take. She walked slowly through the kitchen out to the back patio and the spacious yard.

She spied Sam deep in conversation with Thunder Morgan. Good. Dusty had said how much her brother admired the bronc busting legend. Hopefully that would keep him occupied long enough for her to escape.

Where the heck was Dusty? Sydney walked around looking, purposely avoiding Sam, but her hostess was nowhere to be seen. *Crap.* She'd have to leave without saying goodbye. She hated to do it, but she had no other choice.

She walked back into the house, through the kitchen bustling with caterers preparing food and drink, through the long hallway to the front door.

She stopped abruptly.

Where the heck did she think she was going? Her father had dropped her off and taken the rental car back to Bakersville. She was supposed to call him later to come get her.

God! What a brain fart. She needed to get a grip.

She pulled out her cell phone. The drive from town was over a half hour. She'd have to hole up here and wait for her dad.

"Leaving so soon?"

She jerked and turned. Sam, gorgeous Sam, was standing in the front doorway. Why hadn't she walked farther outside?

"Yes, I'm afraid so," she said, trying to keep her voice from shaking. "I have an early morning."

"Don't we all." He came toward her. "At least have something to eat first. McCray beef can't be beat."

He took her arm. She sucked in a breath. The man's touch could ignite a forest.

"Come on. You can eat with me."

"But you were talking to Mr. Morgan."

"I have all night to talk to Thunder. He's not going anywhere. Right now I'd like to have dinner with you. If you don't mind, that is."

Mind? Was he kidding? She'd love to have dinner with him. Love to spend the whole evening with him. But it wasn't a good idea.

"Well, I—"

"A person's gotta eat, right?" He smiled.

Lord, he was handsome. She relented. "Okay. Dinner sounds good."

His smile broadened. The man had perfect teeth.

They each loaded their plates with food and sat down at a table with Dusty, Zach, and Sean.

Conversation centered around the rodeo, for which Sydney was thankful. Rodeo talk was easy, free of conflict. She could talk rodeo all night and never tire of it. She loved the rodeo.

When dinner was over, Sydney stood. "I'm so sorry. I have an early morning tomorrow so I need to get going. Thank you for having me."

"Can't you stay a little longer?" Dusty asked. "We have a great dessert spread coming up."

"I wish I could, but I need to get home."

Sam stood. "I'll see you out."

"Um...okay." She couldn't be rude, after all.

They walked through the house and out the front door. "Where's your car?" Sam asked.

"I...uh...need to call my father. He dropped me off."

"No problem then. I'll drive you home."

A half hour in Sam's presence? Sounded like heaven, but not a good idea. "Please, you don't need to."

"My pleasure. There's no reason to bother your father."

Energy pulsed between them. Sydney's loins blazed. How could she manage a half hour with him? Refusing was suddenly no longer an option. She wanted to spend another half hour with him. Wanted it so bad she could taste it.

Despite her sweaty palms and speeding pulse, Sydney kept the conversation on the rodeo. Sam was planning to bronc bust in several competitions. Sydney planned to secretly watch. Seeing his physique in action would be pure pleasure.

Sam insisted on seeing her up to her room at the Bakersville Hotel. Her parents and Duke were in a different room, thank goodness.

When they stopped at the door, Sydney's heart fluttered.

Sam grabbed one of her hands. "I want you to know something," he said.

"What?"

"That night we spent, all those years ago, meant a lot to me."

Her tummy tugged. "It did?"

"Yes. I'd hoped it meant something to you too."

Oh, it had. More than he'd ever know. "Yes," she mumbled. "It meant a lot to me."

"I tried to find you once I got back to Montana. But then I got preoccupied with my ranch. It was nearly bankrupt. I'm sorry. I should have kept looking."

She swallowed. She'd lain low for a while. "That's okay. I understand."

"Well—" Sam let out a huff of air. "It's been nice seeing you again."

"Thank you for the ride."

"My pleasure." He shoved his hands in the pockets of his jeans. "I guess I'll see you around the rodeo."

"Yes."

He turned to leave, and Sydney's body quaked. Fierce desire surged through her. Images of their lovemaking five years earlier flashed in her mind. His cock in her mouth, in her body. Orgasm after orgasm after orgasm—

"Sam?"

He turned. "Yes?"

She threw her arms around him and pressed her lips to his.

CHAPTER THREE

Sydney had never been one to shy away from what she wanted. After all, she'd invited him to her room that fateful day. In an instant, desire overcame intellect, and all the reasons she should stay away drifted out on the wings of passion.

Sam's kissing abilities hadn't waned. His lips parted eagerly for her tongue, and his own met hers with a tantalizing sizzle. He tasted of coffee, of spice, of male beauty. A frenzied kiss, just as it had been all those years ago.

She moaned into his mouth, craving more, all of him.

He ripped his mouth from hers and breathed in heavily. "Sweetheart, what are you after?"

She shook her head. "I wish I knew. All I know is that right now I want you. Do you want me as much as I want you?"

"Baby, I want you so bad I think I might die an early death if I can't have you."

Thank God. Quickly she slid her key card through the locking device and opened the door to her room.

They were on each other like mad, ripping their clothes off until garments lay crumpled on the floor in disarray. Naked, they fell onto the bed. He spread her legs and launched into eating her.

It had been so long! To think she'd abstained for five years. *Abstained.*

Why? Had she waited for Sam to come back to her? No, definitely not that. Why had she waited so long? She'd had plenty of opportunities.

His tongue was as talented as she remembered. He tormented her clit, tugged on her folds, teased the entrance to her moist channel.

"Mmm," he said against her, his voice a fuzzy vibration, "you taste so good, sweetheart."

She writhed, grinding against his face. "That feels so damn good, Sam. God, it's been forever."

Had she said that out loud? No matter. This was heaven. She didn't want to worry about saying the wrong thing. She'd just enjoy it.

He pushed her thighs forward and slid his tongue along the crease between her ass cheeks. No one had ever touched her there. Never. Why? It felt amazing. His tongue was silky against that virgin skin.

"Mmm," he said again. "I'd love to take you here sometime."

Her ass? Why was that thought such a turn-on?

"I...don't know—"

"No, baby, not tonight." He pulled her thighs back and set them on his shoulders. His warm brown gaze settled onto hers. "And never without your okay. It's just a thought." He sighed against her skin. "You're just so beautiful, I want all of you."

God, maybe.

Was she actually considering it? The thought aroused her. Icy pinpricks poked at her skin. Something about Sam O'Donovan made her want to do anything and everything to please him. And that thought scared the hell out of her.

Before she could dwell on the thought further, Sam went back to work between her legs. Soon she was flying high, ensconced in a climax so deep she thought she might implode on the spot.

"That's it, sweetheart." He slid his fingers in and out of her. "Come for me. Come for me all night long."

Oh, I will. As the spasms inside her slowed, he bent down and licked her tight bud, and up she flew again. He brought her to orgasm three times, and then four, and when he began a fifth, she pleaded with him to stop.

"I can't take any more, Sam. God, please."

He smiled between her legs, his chin shining with her juices. "Since you asked so nicely."

Déjà vu. He'd used those words before. He got up and grabbed a condom from his jeans, sheathed himself, and thrust into her wetness.

So full, so perfect. How had she gone so long without this wonderful completion? His mouth took hers, and they kissed frantically, passionately, until she had to rip her lips away to take a much-needed breath.

She'd already had multiple orgasms and didn't expect to come again, so the spasms building within her were a welcome surprise.

"I can't believe this. I'm coming again."

"Yeah, baby. Come again for me."

He increased the tempo of his thrusts. "God, yeah," he said. "Oh, God, yeah."

He plunged a final time, and the convulsions of his cock beat against her walls in time with her own climax.

Together they came.

Together they went limp.

"My God," Sam said against her neck.

She couldn't find her voice. Only nodded.

He rolled off her onto the other side of the bed. "It's been a long time."

"For me too," she said. He had no idea how long.

She turned on her side and regarded his gorgeous masculinity. If possible, he'd become even better looking. His sandy brown hair was in shoulder-length disarray, and his warm cognac eyes were heavy-lidded. He was still in the depth of relaxation from his orgasm. His nose was perfectly formed and those lips...too full and pink for a man. Women would spend a bundle on Botox to have them. She couldn't help herself. She leaned over and pressed her mouth to his in a soft kiss.

"That's nice, Syd." He rolled on top of her, pressing his elbows into the bed to keep from crushing her. His gaze pierced hers. "You are beautiful. You haven't changed a bit in five years."

She'd changed. He had no idea. She smiled in spite of herself. "You have. You're even better looking than I remembered."

His cheeks reddened.

She laughed. "You're blushing."

He smiled. "Am not."

"Are too." She lifted her head slightly and kissed his lips again. "Pretty soon your cheeks are going to be as pink as these beautiful lips of yours."

More red. She smiled. This was fun. She reached upward and entwined her fingers through his soft hair. *Mmm, soft as suede.* She inhaled his oaky scent. Fresh as outdoors, just as she recalled.

"It was a wonderful night, wasn't it?" she said.

"Yes." He winked. "You know what, though?"

"What?"

"I'm betting this one will be even better." He crushed his mouth to hers.

★ ★ ★

Sydney woke to the light of dawn streaming through the curtains of her hotel window. She sighed. Colorado mornings were always so beautiful.

Next to her, Sam snoozed on his back, his erection apparent from the tent of the sheets. She gently removed the sheet to view his magnificent body. The satiny bronze of his skin lightened where the streams of sunlight touched it. His cock could have been carved by a Renaissance artist in marble, so perfect it was.

Her sex pulsed just looking at it. She wanted it in her mouth, touching the back of her throat.

Quietly she leaned over and touched her lips to the salty head. She trailed tiny kisses up and down the shaft, licked around his sac.

"Mmm."

She looked up. His eyes were still closed. A slight smile curved the corners of his beautiful lips.

She smiled and bent back to work. She twirled her tongue over his head, savoring the masculine flavor and his husky moans. She took it all until he grazed the back of her throat. She let up, allowing herself to get used to the sensation. It had been a long, long time since she'd done this.

She caressed the hard muscle of his taut thighs as she continued her assault on his beautiful cock. She took him in again to the back of her throat, his moans fueling her desire to please him.

"Sweetheart."

She looked up. His brown eyes were open and locked upon hers. "Yes?"

"If you don't stop now, I'm going to come."

Worked for her. She wanted him to come. She wanted to take him, swallow for him.

Something she'd never done before.

"It's okay. I want you to."

"Oh, God." He closed his eyes.

She continued, and his hips began thrusting upward in time with her oral strokes. Soon the pulses began low on his shaft, and when his fluid shot into her mouth, she took him, relishing the creamy texture, the salty flavor.

"That was amazing," he said when she lay back down beside him.

Happiness flowed through her. "I'm glad you enjoyed it."

He smiled. "I'd be happy to return the favor."

"I'd love it. But I'm famished."

"You want to get room service?"

"They don't have room service here," she said. "We can run up to Rena's and get some coffee and scones or something."

"Hmmm." He rolled over and gazed at her. "Don't really feel like leaving this bed anytime soon."

She laughed. "Neither do I. I think I have some granola bars in my bag. I can make the little pot of coffee too."

He grinned. "Sounds perfect."

After a quick breakfast, he made good on his promise to return the favor and brought her to orgasm twice. Then he thrust into her until they both came so hard, Sydney thought they'd created a sonic boom.

God, sex is good.

No. Sex with Sam *is good.*

Not that she'd know much difference. A high school classmate had taken her virginity in a clumsy coupling. That was the extent of her experience, save for Sam. Didn't much matter anyway. She couldn't have Sam forever, and she'd never want anyone else.

Now they lay together, their arms and legs intertwined, kissing each other sweetly and softly. If she continued kissing him for the next fifty years, she'd never get enough of those soft full lips. They licked each other, made love with their mouths.

A knock on the door startled her. She jerked beneath Sam.

He raised his head. "You want me to get that?"

She shook her head, "No, I'll take care of it." It was probably her mother or father. She couldn't let them find her here with Sam. How would that look?

Course she was over eighteen. Wasn't really their business. But still, they were her parents. They didn't need to see their daughter enjoying the afterglow of incredible sex.

She rose and retrieved her robe from the bathroom. Before she opened the door, she threw Sam his jeans. "Better put these on."

"Okay." He took the jeans. picked up his shirt, and traipsed to the bathroom.

The knocking pounded again. "I'm coming."

When she opened the door, her heart nearly stopped when she saw the familiar face.

"What are you doing here?"

CHAPTER FOUR

Rodney Kyle stood before her, clad in a navy blue business suit. His blond hair was cut above his ears, and his blue gaze penetrated her.

"I missed you."

Her nerves skittered across her skin. *Now what? Sam is in my bathroom, for God's sake.* At least he was getting dressed. What time was it? She had no idea. Dawn had already broken when she awoke.

Rod leaned in for a kiss. She turned her head and his lips slid over her cheek.

"Some greeting," he said.

"I'm sorry, it's just—"

The whoosh of a toilet flush screamed in her ears.

Rod's eyebrows shot up.

"My mother," Sydney said, her voice shaking.

God, Sam, please don't come out of the bathroom!

No such luck. The squeak of the bathroom door brought Sam into the room.

His smile turned downward when he rested his gaze upon Rod. "Uh, who's this, Syd?"

Rod strode forward, brash and businesslike as ever. He held out his hand. "Rod Kyle. Sydney's fiancé."

Sam left Rod's hand in midair. He turned to Sydney. "What the fuck is going on here?"

"This isn't what it looks like," Sydney said.

She wasn't sure which man she was talking do. Did it make a difference?

She wasn't in love with Rod. She'd planned to break if off with him after the rodeo. After she won a purse. Even if she didn't. But how could she get Sam to believe that now?

And how could she explain this to Rod? She'd hoped for an amicable parting. That wouldn't happen now.

Sam, though fully clothed, was clearly disheveled. What would Rod think? Especially since she'd told him she was saving herself for marriage?

And Sam?

She looked like a little slut cheating on her fiancé.

And that's exactly what she had done, her own feelings aside. She should not have slept with Sam while she was still engaged to Rod. She should have broken up with Rod before she came here. She'd meant to. Why hadn't she just grown some guts and done it?

"I'm thinking it's exactly how it looks," Sam said. He took his Stetson from the desk. "Thanks for a good time. I'm outta here." He slammed the door behind him.

"Who the hell is he?" Rod asked.

"A friend. A brother of a friend, actually." At least that was the truth.

Rod grabbed her hand. "Where's your ring?"

"At home. In my safe. You know I don't wear jewelry when I compete."

"A good excuse to leave it home, isn't it?" Rod's lips twitched. "Did he spend the night here?"

How had she made such a mess of things? The last five years had been the most wonderful and the most terrible of her life at the same time.

How had it come to this?

"I asked you a question," Rod said again. "Did he spend the night here?"

Sydney shook, afraid. Rod was not a violent person, at least as far as she knew, but he was a powerful businessman. He could hurt her in worse ways than physically.

She slowly nodded her head.

"I see."

"I'm sorry, Rod."

"Sorry?"

She nodded again. "Yes. I never meant to hurt you."

"Hurt me? You think a little slut like you could hurt me?"

She shuddered. His words shouldn't hurt, but they did. They rang with truth. "I'm afraid I can't marry you." She turned away from his gaze.

"Why not?"

Sydney's neck whipped around. Had she heard right? "Excuse me?"

"I said, why not? You don't think I've been faithful to you all this time, do you? A man has needs. You said you wanted to wait until we were married. Although obviously you got over that last night."

"You mean you—"

"Of course. Don't be naïve. As far as I'm concerned, the engagement can proceed as planned. I never planned on being faithful to you."

She stood, her body numb. "Are you kidding me? This is the kind of marriage you wanted?"

"This *is* marriage, dear. My own parents have been married nearly forty years, and they've both had strings of lovers. My father likes twenty-something blond girls. Ironically, so does my mother."

The reality of the rich—way more information than she wanted. "Rod, I'm really glad I haven't hurt you."

"You don't have the power to hurt me."

"Be that as it may, I'm glad I didn't. But this engagement is over."

"No, it's not."

"I'm sorry, but I'm afraid it is."

He stalked toward her. "The announcements have already been made in all my circles. It is not over."

"But I don't love you."

"I don't love you either."

"Then what's the big deal?"

"You are the kind of wife I need. Beautiful to the eye. From a modest background, so you're attracted to money. You're tall and athletic. You'll bear me strong heirs. You'll be a good hostess."

Anger boiled under her skin. "I'm more than just arm candy, damn it."

"Darling, you are the ultimate arm candy, but I'm afraid that's all you are."

Why did his words cut her? She didn't care, but it still hurt to be spoken of in that manner. "Why does it matter? If that's all I am, I'm easily replaced."

"I'll lose face. And I don't take kindly to that. My parents have gone to a lot of expense and trouble for our impending marriage. Besides, you have value you can't even fathom."

What the hell does that mean? "Your parents are richer than God. They won't care. And I don't care what kind of value you think I have. I'm not marrying you. You can't make me."

Rod shook his head. "Fine. Have it your way."

"Why did you come here?"

"I told you. I missed you."

"That's crap. You just admitted you don't love me. You just wanted to see what was going on. You want to control me."

The man was a control freak in his business. Clearly he was also a control freak in his personal life. How had she gotten involved with him?

Unfortunately, she knew the answer to that question.

Money.

Sydney and her parents were carrying some major debt. Rod had been her savior. But right now, money didn't matter to her. She wanted out.

"I think you'll change your mind. But for now, if we're no longer to be married, I guess I don't have to worry about controlling you."

"That's right. Now get the hell out of here." She pushed him out the door and slammed it shut.

Rod's words stung because they were mean, but not because they'd come from him. That realization made her even more comfortable with her decision to break it off. She hadn't wanted to hurt him, and she hadn't. For that, she was glad.

Now, what to do about Sam?

She couldn't have a life with him. That was out of the question. But she didn't want to hurt him. She didn't want to hurt anyone, but especially not Sam.

She wanted him to know that last night had meant something to her. That their time five years ago had meant something.

That she'd never forgotten him, and she never would.

How, though, could she convey that while also telling him she couldn't see him again?

* * *

How could he have misjudged her?

Sam raked his fingers through his disheveled hair. He needed a shower. He drove up to his small guest house on Zach and Dusty's ranch and took refuge inside.

He inhaled. Pears. Musk. Sex. He could still smell her. Yep, he definitely needed that shower. And it needed to be a cold one. Even now, his cock still throbbed for her.

As the lukewarm water streamed over his tired body, images of Sydney's dark, brooding eyes haunted him. She'd been acting strange yesterday, no doubt. Yet after they'd made love, he'd been sure he imagined it.

No such luck.

The woman was like a disease. She got into his body and wreaked havoc.

The sex had been amazing, though. He connected with her on a level unknown to him with any other woman.

He was tired of trying to replicate the feelings he'd had when he was with Sydney. He'd tried for five years, to no avail. He was done trying.

Sam O'Donovan would live out his life as a bachelor. Yes, he'd always wanted to be a father, but he could still be a father figure. He didn't need his own kids. He'd dote on Seanie and his cousins on Zach's side. Dallas and Annie had four adorable kids, and Chad and Catie had a beautiful little girl named Violet. They all loved their Uncle Sam. Or Uncle Sammy, as Dallas's girls, Sylvie and Laurie, called him.

In a flash, an image of a smiling little boy with sandy brown hair and dark brooding eyes soared into his mind.

His son with the woman he loved.

Loved?

Make that the woman he'd never have.

The child he'd never have.

He let grief consume him for only a few moments. Then he washed his hair, stepped out of the shower, and dried off.

Sam wasn't one to wallow in misery. He'd had his share of it, losing his mother when he was only ten, his father years later. Nearly losing his baby sister. If he'd wallowed in it, he would have had a shitty life.

Still, life had grown stale.

He needed a change. He'd hoped against the odds that Sydney might be that change.

Nope. Not to be.

He dressed quickly and headed over to the main house to see Dusty. She and Zach were sitting at the table, drinking coffee.

"Glad I caught you," Sam said. "I thought you all might have headed over to the grounds already."

"No, not for a few hours yet," Zach said. "Have a seat. Want some coffee?"

"Don't mind if I do. Don't get up. I'll get it." Sam poured himself a cup and sat down next to his sister.

"Rumor has it you left the party with one Sydney Buchanan last night," Dusty said.

"Rumor has it that's none of your business, little sis."

Zach smiled. "Give the man a break, darlin'. You know men don't kiss and tell."

"This isn't a man. He's my brother," Dusty said. "Now spill it."

"There's nothing to spill," Sam said. "I gave her a ride home."

"Now I know darn well you and Chad hooked up with Syd and her friend at the stock show that time. You remember, don't you, Zach?"

"Dust, you're gonna have to give your big brother a break here. He clearly doesn't want to discuss this."

"There's nothing to discuss, and that's final." Truer words had never been spoken. He and Sydney were over. Heck, they'd never begun. Sam took a long drink of the coffee. Good and strong, just as he liked it. "Case closed."

Dusty sighed. "Fine. I understand."

"In that case, Dust and I have something we need to talk to you about," Zach said.

Sam took another sip. "Yeah? What is it?"

"Well, our ranch foreman is retiring, goin' down to Arizona with his family."

"Sorry to hear that."

"We need a new foreman, and Dust and I think you might be the perfect man for the job."

Sam perked up. "I'm listening."

"You wouldn't have to sell the Double D, Sam," Dusty said. "You could have your foreman run it. It's a small operation, and you'll be making more than enough here to keep it running. I know you don't want to sell it. It has sentimental value to both of us."

He set his mug on the table. "I'm not sure it's a good idea to do business with family."

"Which is why I'm offerin' you a cut," Zach said. "That way, you'd be an owner of sorts. Dust and I have discussed this at length with Dallas and Chad and their wives. We all agree you're who we want."

"Plus, it'd be great to have you here, Sam," Dusty added.

A new place. A new job. New challenges. New people to meet, and family to spend time with. It might be just the cure for a life that had grown stale.

Sounded like a gift dropped from heaven.

"I'll definitely give it some thought."

"Please consider it," Dusty said, refilling his coffee. "Zach and I would love to have you here."

"And make no mistake," Zach added, "this ain't nepotism or anything. This was actually my idea, not Dusty's. You are the best man for this job. I don't offer just anyone a share in my ranch, not even my wife's brother. I offer it to you because I know you'll earn it."

Sam opened his mouth to speak, but the doorbell interrupted him.

"Stay put," Dusty said to Zach. "I'll get it."

A few minutes later, Dusty returned with Sydney Buchanan at her side.

Sam's heart leaped.

Then dropped to his belly.

He stood. "I need to get going. Thanks for the coffee."

"Can't you stay for a few more minutes?" Dusty asked.

"Wish I could, Sis, but I've got stuff that can't wait." He grabbed his hat and nodded to Sydney. "Nice to see you again, ma'am."

He walked out the door without looking back.

Too bad his heart was still in the room.

★ ★ ★

"Sit on down," Dusty said to Sydney, "and I'll get you a cup of coffee. You want some coffee cake? Seraphina left a nice one. She took Seanie out for the day."

"Oh, no, thank you." The cake looked delicious but it would taste like sawdust. She couldn't eat right now.

Sam had run from her like an ant from a grasshopper. Not that she blamed him.

She hadn't thought it would cut into her heart like this, though. *Crap*. Of course she had. That was a big ol' lie.

Zach rose. "I'll leave you ladies to your girl talk. Got work to do." He gave Dusty a quick kiss. "See you later, darlin'. And nice to see you, Sydney."

"You too." Sydney sat down and took a sip of the coffee Dusty had given her. "I hope I'm not intruding."

"Not at all. I'm glad to have the company."

"I was hoping we could talk."

"Of course. What's up?"

"I know we don't know each other that well. But really, you're my only friend here. I'm actually surprised you remembered me yesterday."

"How could I forget the woman who beat me in that race?" Dusty smiled.

"You should have won."

"Nah. It turned out the way it needed to turn out. Sometimes it takes a while to see the ultimate plan, but it eventually surfaces."

Does it?

The last five years had been a both a blessing and a hardship. Sydney wasn't sure where she was going next. At least she wasn't marrying Rod. That whole relationship had been a mistake, further evidenced by his visit this morning.

"I'm glad you see it that way."

"I do." Dusty patted Sydney's arm.

The warmth of friendship infused her. Could she really talk to this woman? After all, she was Sam's sister. But she had no one else, and she needed Sam to know the truth. Or at least part of it. She'd start with Dusty.

"I suppose it's no secret that your brother and I met five years ago in Denver."

"Yes, I remember. We all sat together for a few minutes at the Bays' party at the Windsor."

Sydney nodded. "Sam and I, we spent that night together."

Dusty remained silent.

"I hope that doesn't shock you."

"Shock me? Goodness no. I know my brother's not a monk. I just don't really know what to say. But truly, I don't think less of either of you for it."

"Thank you. I appreciate that. The thing is, we hooked up again last night, but..."

"But what?"

"You may think less of me now."

"Why is that?"

"Well, someone showed up this morning and interrupted us."

"Why would that matter?"

"Because of who it was." Sydney cleared her throat. "My fiancé."

Dusty's eyebrows shot up.

"But please believe me," Sydney continued, "Rod and I were over. I was going to break up with him as soon as I got home. In fact, I should have done it sooner. At any rate, it's done now. We broke up this morning."

"He ended it because he found you with Sam?"

"No. Oddly, he was okay with that. If you knew his family,

you'd understand. I was the one who ended it."

"Why?"

"Because I don't love him. I never did. Rod is the heir to a huge hotel business in Carson City. He offered financial security."

Dusty nodded. "I understand."

"You do?"

"Yes, I do. Believe it or not, I was once in financial trouble myself. I know how it feels. I nearly sold my Regina to get money I needed."

"Regina?"

"My barrel racing mare."

"Oh! She's a beautiful horse."

"Thank you. Yes, she is."

Sydney sipped her coffee. "Rod came into my life by accident. I applied for a job at his office. I didn't get it, but I caught his eye. He recognized me from a magazine article on the WPRA. He wanted a woman who had a recognizable name and a good face and body to be arm candy. He also liked the fact that being a barrel racer, I wasn't all that financially secure. That was evident when I applied to work at his company."

"I see. So he asked you out?"

"Yes. It was a whirlwind courtship. I think his daddy told him it was time to get married or something. Within a month, my face was plastered all over the society pages in Carson City. Hotel heir Rodney Kyle and his fiancé, barrel racer Sydney Buchanan. We were the talk of the town."

"Did you love him?"

Sydney shook her head. "No. And I found out today he never loved me either. This was to be solely a business arrangement."

"Do you still need money?"

"Yes, but I'm hoping to win a purse here."

"I think there's a good chance of that."

"I sure hope so." She sighed and took another sip of coffee. "I'm sorry I hurt your brother. I never meant to."

"Sam's a big boy. He'll be okay. Just talk to him."

"That's the thing." Her voice cracked and she steadied it. "I can't talk to him. I can't ever see him again.

CHAPTER FIVE

"That's a good boy." Sam smoothed the jet-black horse's mane.

"He's a beauty, ain't he?"

Sam turned to see Zach. "Yeah, he is. What's his name?"

"Midnight."

"It fits."

Zach nodded. "Want to take him out?"

"I was hoping to, thanks. I need to get out of here for a while."

"Something wrong?"

Sam wasn't one to talk about his problems. He wasn't a woman, for God's sake. But Zach was his brother-in-law and a good friend. "Sydney Buchanan."

"I figured as much, the way you hightailed it out of there this mornin'. What's going on?"

"I suppose it's no secret that she and I hooked up in Denver. You know, back when you and Dusty hooked up."

"Yeah. Did Chad ever tell you about the problems he had with the woman he hooked up with that night? Linda?"

"Yeah. I'm glad that all worked out for the best."

"Me too. Though it came at a rotten time. Right after our ma died."

"I know. I'm sorry." He gave Zach a pat on the back.

"Water under the bridge. Chad's happy as a clam now with Catie."

"I know." Sam chuckled. "I wasn't sure I'd ever see him settle down. He did love the ladies."

"Now he loves one lady. He's as smitten as can be with his wife and baby daughter."

"They're both beauties, that's for sure."

"So what's going on with Miss Buchanan?"

Sam cleared his throat. "Thing is, I'm no Chad McCray, but I've had my share. But that night with Sydney stands out as the best."

"Yeah?"

"I thought maybe I was just having fond memories of my one and only one-night stand. But she and I got together last night, and it was just as good. Better, even."

"And that's bad because...?"

"You don't know the half of it."

"Tell me."

"She's engaged. A little fact she neglected to tell me."

Zach raised his eyebrows. "I don't recall seeing a ring on her finger."

"That's because she wasn't wearing one. But she's engaged to some pretty-boy businessman. He showed up at her hotel room this morning while I was still there."

"How did she explain your presence?"

"I haven't the foggiest. Didn't stick around to find out."

"Well, if you want to know what's going on, go on up to the house. She's having coffee with Dust."

Sam shook his head. "Can't. She flat out lied to me. Who has sex with another man when she's engaged? That's crazy shit."

"Maybe there's an explanation."

"What kind of explanation can there possibly be?" Sam

shoved his hands in his pockets. "We had great sex. Twice. But great sex doesn't make up for a lack of trust."

"Are you looking for something with this girl?"

"I thought I might be. Hell, I don't know. Life's gotten kind of boring, Zach. Which is why"—he took a few steps forward and held out his hand—"I've decided to take you up on your offer. Coming here to Colorado, being near my sister and nephew, might be just what the doctor ordered."

Zach shook his hand. "Good. We're all thrilled to have you on board here at McCray Landing. When can you start?"

"After the rodeo, I'll head back to Montana to make sure the Double D is taken care of. I think I can persuade my foreman to take over. Once things are settled, I'll get down here as soon as I can."

"Would you like to see the house for the foreman?" Zach asked. "It's vacant. You can move in anytime."

"I'd love to."

"Good. You saddle up Midnight there, and I'll get Attila ready. We can ride on over and take a look at it."

Yes, this would be just what he needed. Once the rodeo was over and Sydney Buchanan went back to Nevada, he could concentrate on starting his new life.

★ ★ ★

Dusty's mouth dropped open. "What do you mean you can't see Sam again?"

Sydney's heart ached. Sam was amazing, and such a nice man. And she adored Dusty and her little boy.

God, her little boy.

Some hurts never healed.

"It's not something I can talk about."

"I guess I don't see the problem. You broke up with your fiancé. You're a free woman now."

"But I neglected to tell Sam I was engaged."

"So?"

"Well...we spent last night together."

"You told me that. And yes, the guy showed up. But you can just explain to Sam that you were planning to break up with him, which is the truth."

"Still—"

"My big brother is a great guy, Syd. If he's interested in you, don't let him go."

"I don't want to."

"Then don't. Whatever's going on, be honest with him. If he cares for you, and I think he does, he'll help you. He was there for me all those years when I needed him. He sacrificed his own happiness so I was taken care of."

Sydney nodded. She'd known for a while that Dusty had been ill when she was younger. "Your leukemia."

"Yeah. It's also the reason I can't have more children. It left me nearly infertile. Sean was a gift from heaven."

"Oh, Dusty, I had no idea. I'm so sorry." Here she was complaining. How selfish could she be?

"Don't be. I'm fine now. I'm ten years out and considered cured. But my point is Sam was there for me when I needed him. He took care of me. My father passed away during that time, and Sam was all I had. So when I tell you he's a special man, I'm not just saying that because he's my brother."

Sydney looked at her lap. Sam *was* wonderful. She'd always known that. Sometimes she looked back at her life and wondered why she'd made the decisions she had.

Perhaps he'd forgive her for not telling him she was engaged.

But other things could never be forgiven.

"I'm sorry to keep you so long," Sydney said, rising. "I need to get to the rodeo and warm Sapphire up. I've got a race this afternoon."

Dusty took her hand. "I'm glad you came over. Whatever is bothering you, I promise it will work out. Trust me, I've hit rock bottom before and come out swinging. You will too."

Sydney wasn't so sure, but she smiled halfheartedly. "Thanks."

"And I'll be there cheering you on in the stands this afternoon. Good luck."

"Thanks. That means a lot." She walked out the door and drove away.

★ ★ ★

Sydney took a deep breath and smoothed Sapphire's soft white mane. She hadn't hit her personal best of 14.1 in seven years. She was last to go in the competition, which only made her more tense. But at least she knew what she was up against. So far, the fastest time belonged to a local girl at 14.5. She could still take first, but it would require intense concentration and perfect form.

She had to win. She needed the money. Especially now that Rod was out of the picture for good.

One more deep breath and she closed her eyes. In her mind, she and Sapphire ran like the wind, skating around every barrel with perfect ease.

She opened her eyes, signaled to the judge, and then kicked

into high gear. She and Sapphire crossed the electric eye and raced toward the first barrel. Sydney clenched her teeth as she set the mare up to turn the first barrel without knocking it over. Then, in a whirlwind, Sydney took Sapphire around the first barrel perfectly. Pursing her lips, she looked straight ahead and galloped toward the second, taking Sapphire around in the opposite direction. Excellent. One more to go. Running toward the backside of the arena, she and the mare aimed toward the third and final barrel, the sweet rush of adrenaline empowering her.

Yes, yes, she was doing it! Sapphire was in fine form as she rounded the last barrel.

Thundering applause echoed from the stands. She ignored it. Only the race mattered. She and Sapphire were alone in the universe. Alone to conquer the world.

A microsecond later, Sapphire rounded the final barrel and they headed back down the center of the arena.

She crossed the electric eye but didn't see her time.

Had she made it?

Had she beaten 14.5?

She didn't know. But right now it didn't matter. Sapphire had worked hard and needed Sydney's attention. She dismounted and petted the mare's nose. "Great job, sweetie."

Within a few seconds, the local girl, Sandra something or other, approached her. "Good race."

"You too."

"Congratulations. Fourteen-three is a great time. "

I won? Warmth flooded her. "Thank you."

"It's a fine purse you'll be getting."

"Congratulations to you, too. You had a great score."

Sandra smiled. "Thank you. See you next race."

Sydney's heart leaped. She'd done it! Not her personal best, but as close as she'd gotten in seven years. All those hours working with Sapphire had paid off.

She led the mare to the grooming area and got to work. Soon her parents and Duke joined her.

"That was great, Sassy!" her little brother exclaimed.

Sydney smiled. When Duke had been learning to talk, he couldn't say Sydney, so he called her Sassy. It had stuck. Though he was five, they all still used the nickname. She pulled the little boy into her arms and kissed his apple-red cheek. He was such a beauty, with light brown hair and dark walnut eyes.

"One day you'll be the best bronc buster in the world."

Duke turned to his mother. "Can't I please do the mutton busting, Mama?"

"You're still a little too young," his mother replied.

"I'm five. I'm allowed."

"Now we promised Mama you wouldn't do it till you were six, " Sydney said. "Next year will come soon enough."

"It's bad enough I had to watch you and Blake fall off animals and nearly kill yourselves when you were older than Duke. Let me keep my baby for one more year."

All the talk meant nothing to Duke, who sulked in Sydney's arms.

"Don't worry, partner." His father patted his head. "You'll be big enough next summer."

"Sydney!" Dusty ran forward, dragging Sean by the hand. "You were incredible. Congratulations!"

"Thank you," Sydney said. Her nerves ricocheted. Now what? It would be rude not to introduce her family. "These are my parents, Roy and Carrie Buchanan, and this is my baby brother, Duke."

"It's wonderful to meet you." Dusty held out her hand. "I'm Dusty McCray, and this is my son, Sean."

"One of the infamous McCrays." Roy Buchanan smiled. "Great to meet you."

"I'm so sorry we missed you at our gathering last night."

"Yes, well—" Roy cleared his throat. "Duke here wasn't feeling all too well, but he's much better now."

"I'm glad. He and Seanie look about the same age. We'd love you to bring him over while you're in town. I'm sure they'd get along great."

"Thank you so much for the offer," Carrie said. "We'll take you up on it if there's time."

"Even if you can't, we're having another big party at the end of the rodeo. If you're still in town, you must come."

Sydney fidgeted. Why did Dusty have to have another party?

Before Sydney could formulate an excuse not to attend, Dusty spoke again. "There's my brother. Sam! Over here!"

Good God, no.

Sam loped up, black Stetson on his head, his sandy hair curling along the outside. His gorgeous physique was apparent in his black western shirt and dark denim jeans. Was that the outline of his sculpted abs under the shirt? Sydney's heart raced.

Sam smiled.

It wasn't a real smile. It looked pasted on.

"Good afternoon." He removed his hat.

"Sam, these are Sydney's parents, Roy and Carrie," Dusty said. "And this gorgeous little creature is Duke."

"You have a little brother?" he said to Sydney.

She looked down. "Yes."

"He's a mighty fine-lookin' young man."

"Thank you," Duke said with a smile.

"I'm sure you're right proud of your big sister." He turned to Sydney. "That was an amazing race."

Her cheeks warmed. "Thank you." She turned. "If you'll excuse me, I need to take care of Sapphire."

"Of course," Dusty said. "We'll see you later." She and Sam walked off, Sean in tow.

"We'll meet you down by the concessions," Roy said, taking Duke.

"Okay, I'll be there in about half an hour, soon as I get her settled."

A few minutes later she was currying Sapphire. Her mare was beautiful, pure white. She'd wondered, when she bought her, why the previous owner had named her Sapphire.

No longer. The name fit. The mare was a jewel.

"Hello."

She turned toward the deep timbre. She didn't have to. She knew exactly who it was.

Sam O'Donovan.

She cleared her throat. "Hello."

"Congratulations again on the race."

"Thank you." She went back to work on Sapphire. "Is there something you wanted?"

"Yes."

She looked back up at him. Why did he have to be such a beautiful man?

And why couldn't her heart stop pounding?

"What?" she asked.

"This."

He stalked forward, grabbed her, and crushed his mouth to hers.

CHAPTER SIX

Sydney couldn't let this happen. She knew that, in her rational mind.

Problem was, her rational mind didn't control this part of her.

Right now she wanted this kiss. Wanted Sam with an astounding passion that surprised even her.

When he ripped his mouth from hers, she whimpered at the loss, but his nips and kisses on the nape of her neck soothed her.

"Oh God," she whispered.

"I want you," he said against her neck. "I want you so much."

"I want you too."

Sam pressed his mouth on hers again. The kiss was demanding this time, almost punishing. He took from her, marked her.

When he paused to take a breath, his gaze penetrated her. For a second, she could actually feel it boring beneath her skin.

"Why?" he said. "Why didn't you tell me?"

Her tummy plummeted. "What?"

"That you were engaged? I thought we had something special. Last night was just as amazing as it was five years ago. Can you stand there and tell me you didn't feel something?"

She gulped. Shook her head. "I felt a lot. I... You have no idea how much I felt."

"Why did you do it?"

She averted her gaze. "I don't know."

That was a lie. She *did* know. She could at least tell him that much.

He cupped her cheek and returned her gaze to his. "Look at me, damnit."

"I'm sorry," she choked out. "I *do* know why I did it. I did it because I wanted you. Because I've never forgotten what it was like with you."

"But your fiancé—"

"Is gone. I broke up with him this morning."

"Don't you mean he broke up with you? I'm sure you had a hell of a time explaining who I was."

"Actually, no. I did the breaking up. I had planned to do it before I came here but I didn't. I'm not sure why. But I did it this morning. He was willing to forget the whole thing."

Sam arched his eyebrows. "What?"

"That's the kind of guy he is. It was never going to be a marriage in the real sense. I never even had sex with him."

"What?" Sam said again.

"I never had sex with him. I told him I was saving myself for marriage. I haven't had sex with anyone since—" She clamped her hand over her mouth.

"Since when, Sydney?" Sam gripped her shoulders. "What are you trying to say to me here?"

The truth burst from her lips. "Since *you*, damnit! I haven't had sex since that night with you five years ago."

His brown eyes smoked. "Is your horse taken care of?"

"Yes. I just finished."

"Good. You're coming with me."

★ ★ ★

Sam's lovemaking was forceful, as though he were marking her, making her his.

Yet it was wonderful at the same time. Sydney wanted to be his. Wanted the passion and desire she'd only experienced with this man.

Could she dare have it?

As she straddled atop him, his cock embedded deep inside her, his fingers pulling her hard nipples, she thought, for an instant, that it could work.

He wanted her. That was obvious.

"Ride me, sweetheart. Just like that."

His deep voice was so sexy.

"God yes, Sam, I love how you feel inside me."

"I love it when you talk like that, baby. You make me hard." His hips rose from the bed and he pushed farther into her.

Sydney reached down to her own special spot and began rubbing in time with Sam's upward thrusts.

"Yeah, sweetheart, you're so hot when you touch yourself there. God, you're beautiful."

"You're beautiful too, Sam. So gorgeous. I've never seen a more beautiful man."

He thrust into her. "Never like this. Never before or after you."

He had no idea. "Amazing with you. Only with you."

"I'm gonna come, baby." He thrust harder.

As his shaft pulsed within her, her own orgasm blasted through her veins like boiling honey.

So good. So right.

Could she have this? Could it work?

They hadn't said a word as they rushed to her hotel room. It wasn't far from the rodeo arena. He'd dragged her by the hand up to the room and nearly thrown her on the bed. Frantically they'd stripped each other, and within seconds she was on top of him, impaled on him.

Now she slid off him, mourning the loss of his cock. She lay down next to him.

He propped up on one shoulder and looked at her. "We need to talk."

Oh God. She waited.

He cleared his throat. "I want to be able to trust you."

"I know."

"You should have told me you were engaged."

"You're absolutely right. And I shouldn't have gone to bed with you while I was engaged to someone else, even if I was intending to end it."

"You're right."

"This isn't an excuse, but...I couldn't resist you, Sam. I couldn't resist you five years ago, and I couldn't now. I'm not afraid to go after what I want, but I'm not the type who goes around having one-night stands."

"You invited me to your room that night, Sydney."

"I know. And it wasn't like me at all. There was something about you."

He nodded. "I understand, believe it or not. I never believed in chemistry before. I never believed in love at first sight."

Her heart lurched. "Love at first sight?"

"I'm sorry. I don't want to scare you."

Adrenaline spiked through her. "I'm not scared, just a little confused. What exactly are you saying?"

"We know little about each other, but I can tell you one thing. I have never in my life felt the way I do when I'm with you."

"Neither have I."

"Then is it love we're feeling?"

"I don't know."

"From my end, it sure seems to be."

Warmth flooded her. Did he truly love her? Could it possibly happen? Even with everything else she hadn't told him yet?

He caressed her cheek. "I love you, Sydney."

She shouldn't say it back. It would just make things harder, but the words tumbled off her tongue. "I love you too, Sam. God, I love you so much."

She meant the words with all her heart.

It was now or never. She had to level with him. He deserved the truth. She might lose him, but she could no longer live the lie.

"Sam, I need to tell you something."

"What is it, baby?"

A knock on the door interrupted her. "Who could that be? I know Mom and Dad were keeping Duke at the rodeo to watch the rest of the events. He already had his nap before my race."

"Whoever it is, get rid of him," Sam said, pressing his lips to hers. "I want you back in this bed."

She smiled. Saved by the knock. For now at least. She pulled on her robe and opened the door.

"Hello, darling Sydney," Rod Kyle said.

"What are you doing here?"

He pushed past her and walked into the room. Sam, still naked, jumped to his feet.

"For God's sake, put some clothes on," Rod said, turning his head.

Sam hurried into his jeans. "What's going on, Sydney? I thought you two were over."

"We are. Why are you here, Rod?"

"I did a little digging today, and I found some stuff that I thought you might find interesting."

"Nothing you have to say interests me," she said. "Now leave, please."

"Not until I say what I came to say."

"You heard the lady," Sam said. "Get the hell out of here."

Rod was no match for muscular Sam. Yet he didn't seem fazed.

"You and your friend here might be interested in this." He handed a paper to Sydney.

She gulped. "Oh God."

"What is it?" Sam ripped the document out of her hands.

He scanned the paper. "A birth certificate. Baby Boy Buchanan? With you as the mother?"

Her heart sank. Now he knew the truth, and it wouldn't take long for him to put two and two together.

"September first? Five years ago? And you haven't had sex with anyone since me?" He stalked toward her. "Goddamnit, you had my baby, and I never even knew it!"

CHAPTER SEVEN

Rod smiled a smug grin. "This just keeps getting better. I didn't expect this turn of events. I just thought you had a child when you were a young maid of nineteen."

"Nineteen?" Sam reddened. "You were only nineteen? That makes you twenty-four now?"

"Nearly twenty-five. Next month, in fact."

"Christ." Sam raked his fingers through his hair. "Where is he? Where is my son?"

She trembled, tried to keep her voice calm. "He was put up for adoption."

"Why didn't you contact me? I would have helped. I would have taken the child. I would have—" He plunked down on the bed, his eyes wet and sunken. "I've always wanted kids."

Sydney ran to him and touched his cheek.

He pushed her hand away. "Don't touch me."

"Sam, I love you."

"I don't want to hear that right now."

Her heart breaking, she rose and stalked toward Rod. "Why did you do this? I mean nothing to you. You admitted that this morning."

"I don't like being rejected. Rodney Kyle doesn't get rejected, certainly not by the likes of you."

"I was only some stupid trophy wife to you," Sydney said. "Why does it matter?"

"You're the wife I want, and I mean to have you."

"Too bad. You can't have me. You think you can show up with this birth certificate and turn my life upside down? And I'll take you back?"

"You might. If you want to keep this little tidbit of news from getting out."

Clearly he didn't know everything. She'd have to tread carefully.

"Why should I care if it gets out?"

"I can see there's a problem with my plan. I thought perhaps you'd want to keep the news from the father. I had no idea I'd find the actual father in your bed."

Sam finally spoke. "Don't talk about me like I'm not here, asshole." He stood. "I'll make you a deal, Kyle. You're obviously good at finding information. Find out where my child is, and I won't smash your face into this wall."

Sydney froze. *Oh God.*

"Should be easy enough," Rod said. "I'll get right to it. I do value my face, after all. But not until Sydney agrees to reinstate our engagement."

Sydney looked pleadingly at Sam.

"What?" His eyes flashed anger. Rage. "I don't give a fuck what you do. You gave away my child."

Nausea crept into her throat. How could this be happening? "You just said you love me."

He sniffed. "I'll get over it." He put on his shirt and boots and grabbed his hat.

He went to the desk and scribbled something on a piece of hotel stationery. He handed it to Rod. "Here's my name and number. Find my kid. If I don't hear from you within twenty-four hours, I swear to God I'll hunt you down and kick your ass into next year."

He put his hat on and left.

"What will it take for you not to find the kid?" she asked Rod.

"Since I have no desire to have that Neanderthal pummel me, I don't see why I shouldn't acquiesce to his request. What do you care? Don't you want to know where your son is?"

What could she say to that? "It's not that I don't want to know. I just can't dredge up that part of my life. It's too painful."

"What will you do for me? Marry me?"

God no, she couldn't. She loved Sam. *Damn it, I love Sam so much.*

"I'm sorry. I can't marry you, Rod. For the life of me, I don't know why you want me."

"This is a blemish, that's no lie. I don't relish having bastard half siblings of my own flesh and blood running around."

"See? Good. You don't want to marry me."

"So there's no reason not to honor the man's request, is there? He has a right to know where his child is."

Sydney clenched her fists, her heart pounding. "Damn you! Why do you want to do this? Why are you trying to hurt me?"

Rod smiled sardonically. "Because I can."

She pushed him out the door and slammed it. He was pure evil. How had she gotten involved with the likes of him?

Money.

It all came down to money.

The purse she won today would help. They weren't destitute after all, but the small Buchanan ranch needed help. Right now they were being forced to sell off their livestock, and a ranch couldn't exist without its stock.

Her big brother, Blake, had abandoned them long ago, but

she would not. Her parents deserved better. Duke deserved better.

Duke.

Such an angel.

She walked to the bathroom and took off the robe. She needed a shower.

★ ★ ★

Goddamn her to hell!

Sam drove back to the rodeo at top speed.

Once there, he walked through the crowds, looking for Sydney's parents. He'd find out once and for all what the hell was going on.

Maybe they didn't even know she'd had a child.

Well, too bad. Today they'd find out. If they had any information about his kid, they were damn well going to give it to him.

God, where were they? The damn place was so fucking crowded.

"Hey, Sam!"

Crap. Dusty. He loved his baby sister, but he did not have the time right now.

"What is it, Dust?"

"Did you have a chance to talk to Sydney?"

What was that about? "I don't have any desire to talk to her."

"Listen, she told me all about her engagement. She's not in love with that guy, and she was going to break up with him anyway. Did you know they never even had sex?"

"I don't care right now. I'm sorry, Dust, but I'm busy."

"You don't care? You don't seem like you don't care whenever you're with her. The chemistry between you two is palpable."

He looked above Dusty's red-gold head, scanning for the Buchanans. "The chemistry between us, if it's even there, is not any of your business. Right now I have to find some answers."

"Answers about what?"

He turned and faced his sister. What the hell? She'd find out anyway. "About my child, Dusty. Sydney had my child five years ago and gave it up for adoption."

Dusty's eyes widened. "What?"

"It's true. I just found out."

"You mean Seanie has a cousin? Who's almost his exact age?"

"Yes, Sis, that's exactly what it means. Where's that genius IQ of yours today? This isn't rocket science."

"I need to sit down." Dusty visibly trembled.

He took his sister's arm and found a bench with one empty spot. "Stay here," he said. "I'm sorry. I didn't mean to upset you. But right now I need to find Sydney's parents."

"Give me a minute," Dusty said. "I know where they are. I saw them a while ago. They're in the stands."

"Where?"

"To the north."

"Thanks, Sis. I'll go find them."

"I want to go with you."

"I need to do this alone. I'll tell you what I find out."

His heart beat like a drum against his sternum. A child. He had a child.

A son.

A little boy.

What might he look like?

A mini Sam? A mini Sydney? A combination?

He made his way to the north stands and scanned the crowd. *Damnit, where are they?*

And then he spied them, Roy and Carrie, with little Duke sitting between them. He sprinted up the stairs, nearly knocking over a hot dog vendor.

"I need to talk to you two," he said.

"Goodness," Carrie said. "Oh, yes, you're Dusty's brother."

"Yes. Sam O'Donovan. I want some answers."

"Answers about what?" Roy said.

"About my son. Where the hell is my son?"

Carrie's pretty face, so like Sydney's, whitened. "Roy—"

"I'll take care of this, Carrie." He turned to Sam. "Come with me, and we'll talk."

"No," Carrie said, "I'm coming with you."

"You stay here."

"No, damnit. I'm coming with you." She stood up and lifted her son into her arms. "Let's get the hell out of here."

Finding a quiet place to talk was nearly impossible, but they found a spot where the noise wasn't so loud. Carrie sat down on a bench with Duke, and Roy took Sam around a corner and lowered his voice.

"Now, young man, what's this about?"

"Your future son-in-law, Rod Kyle, came by with some news today. It seems Sydney had a baby five years ago."

He didn't seem surprised. Clearly he already knew.

"Yes. And?"

"I happen to be the child's father."

Roy's eyebrows shot up. "Are you sure? She never told us who it was."

"Why wouldn't she tell you?"

"She probably didn't want us to go hunting you down."

Sam forced his teeth to unclench. "I wish she would have. I want my child."

"He's been adopted into a loving home."

"How do you know?"

"It was an open adoption."

"Then you know who has him. Tell me."

He shook his head. "I can't."

"Why not?" He grabbed the collar of Roy's shirt. "Damnit. I have a right to know where my child is!"

Roy stared into Sam's eyes. "I'm sorry, son. I can't give you any information."

"Why not?"

"Because he's with parents who love him very much. If you do anything to challenge that relationship, the only person harmed will be your son. The parents will suffer, but the child will be the ultimate loser."

"Damnit!" Sam punched the wall. His fist went through the drywall. His knuckles bled, yet he felt no pain.

No pain at all.

Only anger.

At Sydney.

At Roy.

At Carrie.

He walked away from Roy and turned the corner. Sydney's mother sat with Duke. He was a beautiful child. He had Sydney's eyes.

And sandy brown hair.

Oh my God. Was it possible?

He left Roy standing and stalked toward the woman and

child. He eyed Duke up and down. Could it be?

When he noticed the little boy's hands, his heart nearly leaped out of his chest.

They were tiny replicas of his own.

CHAPTER EIGHT

Carrie shielded the child against her chest. "Back away," she warned.

Sam steeled himself. He had to think of Duke.

Roy strode forward. "Sam, what are you doing?"

"You were right in the first place," he ground out, trying his damndest to stay calm, to not alarm the child. *His* child. "We need to speak alone."

"Take Duke back to the hotel, Carrie," Roy said calmly.

"But the car... How will you—"

"I'll find a ride. Just go. Now."

Carrie stood and ushered Duke away.

Roy sank down on the bench that they had vacated. "Do you really want to turn his life upside down?"

Sam grabbed Roy by the collar again, bringing him to his feet and slamming his back into the wall. "You have turned *my* life upside down, goddamnit."

"I am sorry." Roy's dark eyes misted. "Let go of me, please."

"Why should I?"

"Because I didn't know he was yours. Sydney never told us."

She didn't? Sam let go and pushed Roy back down on the bench. "Now start talking. You owe me that much."

"She was young, only nineteen. She was a champion racer. She couldn't keep a child."

"So what? Maybe I could have."

"She never told us who you were. I think because she knew we'd try to contact you. Carrie and I always felt the father had a right to know."

"Why wouldn't she tell you?"

"I don't know. That's something you'll have to ask her."

"I'm never speaking to her again. So you'll have to tell me."

Roy shook his head. "I told you. I don't know."

"How did you end up with him?"

"Sydney was too young to take care of a child. But she didn't want to give him up. Carrie and I were becoming empty nesters. Blake had left while Sydney was pregnant, and Syd was nineteen and ready to fly on her own. We were still young enough to be good parents. It made sense."

"Well, it doesn't make sense to me."

"We love him as our own. He's our child, and our biological grandchild. He's had a good life. He's happy."

"What makes you think he wouldn't have been happy with me?" Sam's voice cracked.

"Maybe he would have. I don't know. But did you want to raise a child alone? Your son has a mother and father who adore him and a big sister who couldn't love him more."

"And when were you planning to tell him that his big sister is actually his mother?"

"I don't know." Roy sighed. "Eventually we did plan to tell him."

"I want to spend some time with him."

"That's not possible."

"I'll drag your asses to court, then. The kid is my flesh and blood."

"Are you absolutely sure he's yours?"

"Are you kidding? Take a good look at me."

Roy perused him and nodded soberly.

"And even if we looked nothing alike, I have further proof. Sydney has admitted to me that she hasn't been with anyone since we were together five years ago. He has to be mine."

"Thank God."

"Thank God? Are you kidding?"

"You don't understand. I mean thank God she didn't sleep with that slime Rodney Kyle."

"She broke up with him today."

"Thank God again. She was only with him for his money."

"She needs money?"

"Our ranch isn't doing very well. It's the economy and all."

Sam understood. God knew he'd been there. He'd only gotten the Double D out of trouble in the last couple years. But damnit, he didn't want to feel sorry for these people.

They'd stolen his child, for God's sake.

"I'm sorry," he said, despite his anger.

"Sydney didn't want the ranch to go under," Roy continued. "She wanted it for Duke. The ranch has been In the Buchanan family for three generations."

"I want a DNA test, pronto."

"I won't put him through that."

"Fine." Sam stopped himself from putting his fist through the wall again. Wasn't easy. "I'll get a court order. Then you won't have a choice."

"Do you really want to do this to the child?"

"What about me? Don't I have rights?"

Roy nodded. "Of course you do. But he's five years old. He's secure in his life, his family."

"Why didn't anyone try to find me?"

"I told you. Sydney never told us who the father was."

"Why the hell not?"

"You'll have to ask her that."

"I plan to ask her plenty. So much for never speaking to her again." He took off his hat and raked his fingers through his hair—hair just like Duke's. His son. "Where the hell is she?"

"I don't know."

He'd left her at the hotel. He didn't want to see her, but she was the only one who could answer these questions.

She was the last person he wanted to see.

And the first person he wanted to see.

Goddamnit.

He loved her.

How had it come to this?

Yes, his life had gotten stale. He'd wanted to shake things up. But not like this.

He left Roy and walked out of the arena toward the parking area.

And who should be walking toward him, but sharply dressed businessman Rod Kyle.

"Ah, Mr. O'Donovan, just the man I was looking for. I've found your answer for you, and even *you* won't believe where your son is."

"He's here in town." Sam gritted his teeth. "He's Sydney's little brother." Then he hit Rod square in the jaw. Felt damn good, even with bleeding knuckles.

Rod fell backward, rubbing his face. "Hey, we had a deal."

"The deal was you find out where my son is."

"I did."

"Not quick enough. I figured it out without you. Now get the hell out of my sight before I do some real damage."

Sam found his rental car and drove away. The rodeo was

still going on, but Zach's brother Dallas would be home. Dallas didn't compete like his two younger brothers. He was a shooter at heart. He'd be at the ranch. It was near suppertime.

Dallas was one of the only two attorneys in Bakersville. The other was Chad's brother-in-law, Harper Bay, but he was busy planning a wedding in less than a week. Dallas was Sam's best bet.

He drove to Dallas and Annie's ranch house on the McCray property, walked up, and knocked.

"Hello there, Sam," Annie McCray said in her biting Jersey accent. "Nice to see you."

"Is Dallas at home?"

"Yeah, he sure is. Come on in. We're just finishing our dinner."

"I'm sorry to intrude. I have a legal problem."

"No intrusion. Let me get the kids out of your way, and you and he can talk. Come on in to the kitchen."

After they said hi to their Uncle Sammy, Annie took Sylvie and Laurie by the hands and escorted them into the family room where the babies were sleeping in their bassinets. "Sam's here to see you, hon. Legal talk."

"What can I do you for, Sam?" Dallas asked, standing. "You want to sit down?"

"Do I ever." Sam plunked his ass in a chair.

"Coffee?"

"Got anything stronger?"

Dallas smiled. "That bad, huh? How about a Macallan, neat?"

"Sounds like nectar of the gods."

Dallas poured two drinks and sat back down at the table. "So what's going on?"

"I need to get a court order for a DNA test."

"What for?"

"You know the Buchanans, right?"

"Blake and Sydney, yeah. And their parents are here for the rodeo too."

"Along with their little boy. He's about Sean's age."

"Duke, yeah. I've seen him."

"Well, here's the thing." He cleared his throat. "Little Duke Buchanan is my son."

★ ★ ★

"Well, Sydney," Roy Buchanan said when Sydney opened the door to her hotel room. "You've got yourself in quite a mess now."

"I know, Daddy." She sniffed.

"You've been crying."

"Of course I have."

"Tell me what's going on."

"It's that jerk, Rod. He found Duke's birth certificate. He brought it over here and confronted me while Sam was here. Sam put two and two together and figured out he was the father."

"Sam O'Donovan. A good man from a good family. Why didn't you tell us who the father was?"

"I had my reasons. Don't worry, Daddy, he doesn't know where the child is. But I'm afraid he will soon. He asked Rod to find out for him."

"Rod's quick, then. Or Sam figured it out on his own. He confronted your mother and me this afternoon at the rodeo."

Sydney cringed, resisting the urge to swat away the

invisible insects crawling on her skin. "Oh, Daddy. What are we going to do?"

Roy sat down and cupped his head in his hands. "I don't know, Sydney. I just don't know."

"I can't let anything happen to Duke."

"Good, I'm glad to hear you say that. Duke is the most important thing here. We must consider what's best for him first and foremost."

"Of course." Sydney's blood turned to ice. "That's what I've always done."

"Not always, Sydney."

"What do you mean?"

"Why didn't you tell us back then who the father was? Then maybe all this turmoil could have been avoided. Sam would have known. He would have had a choice to be in Duke's life."

"I didn't want him in Duke's life."

"Why, Sydney? Why didn't you want the father to know about his child?"

★ ★ ★

"I see," Dallas said after Sam had explained the situation. "All this time you never knew he existed."

"Not at all."

"And had you known at the time, would you have wanted the child?"

Sam rose, shoved his hands in his pockets. "How the hell should I know? That was over five years ago. I know I want him now."

"Why do you want him now?"

"I've always wanted kids. Just never found the right woman."

"And is Sydney Buchanan the right woman?"

He sat back down with a plunk. "I don't know. Shit, a mere five hours ago I was sure she was."

"Are you in love with her?"

"I was five hours ago, before all this shit hit the fan."

"You have a child with the woman you love." Dallas smiled. "That's a beautiful thing. The rest can be worked out."

"Dallas, my child is five years old! I've missed a half decade of his life. I didn't hear his first word. I didn't see his first smile, his first step."

"I understand." Dallas looked toward the family room where the girls were playing. "Believe me, I understand."

"I have rights, damnit. I want to know my son."

"The child legally belongs to the Buchanans. They adopted him. I'm assuming they went through all the legal channels."

"What if they didn't?"

"I suppose it's possible that Sydney just let her parents raise him."

"She said she was only nineteen when she had him. I can't believe she was that young when we met. She seemed so much older. She was a champion barrel racer. Dusty was twenty-three at that time."

"And you were?"

"Twenty-seven. I feel like I robbed the cradle."

"She was legal, Sam. You didn't do anything wrong."

"I know that." He shook his head. Emotion coursed through him. "Damnit!"

"First thing is to find out if the Buchanans *are* Duke's legal parents. If they are, this is going to be more difficult. I won't lie to you. If they're not, and Sydney is the legal parent, it will be easier for you to get paternal rights."

"Can you find that out?"

"Where was the child born?"

"Hell if I know. Nevada, probably." Sam took a drink of Scotch. "That's where they live now."

"That's a start. We can search the records."

"How long will that take?" Sam asked.

"I don't have an office. I'm not a practicing lawyer. I'll have to call someone in Denver. But there's an easier way to get this information."

"And what might that be?"

Dallas cleared his throat. "Ask Sydney."

"Are you kidding? She's hardly proved herself trustworthy. First, she neglected to tell me she was engaged to some effeminate businessman, and now this? I'm not taking her word for anything."

"All right. Fair enough. Her parents, then."

"I doubt they'll cooperate. I was pretty hard on Roy at the rodeo."

"I'm sure he understands. This is a lot for you to deal with."

Sam nodded. Finally, someone who understood, or at least tried to. "They see me as a threat. They're probably afraid I'm going to take Duke."

"Are you?"

"I just might. He is mine, after all. I was never given a choice in the matter."

"How do you think that would affect them?"

Sam clenched both his fists in his unruly hair. "It'll hurt.

I know that. This isn't their fault. According to Roy, Sydney never told them who the father was."

"Hmm. Why didn't she?"

"Do you honestly think I have a clue? I don't know anything about that woman."

"Only that you love her."

"Love her?" He unclenched his hair. "She's a completely different woman than the one I thought I loved earlier today."

"I see."

"So what are my chances? What do I need to do?"

"We can get a court order for a DNA test, but that's not your main problem."

"The DNA will show he's mine. Sydney admitted to me that she hadn't been with anyone since she was with me over five years ago, and the child was born after that. Plus, have you seen him? He's definitely my son."

"Have you told Dusty?"

"No. I haven't told anyone. Just you."

Dallas sighed. "I feel for you, I really do. But like I said, there's a bigger problem than proving that he's yours."

"What's that?" Sam asked.

"Whenever a child is involved, the courts focus on one thing and one thing only—the best interests of the child in question."

"How can I not be in his best interest? I'm his father."

"He's a child of five. The only parents he's ever known are the Buchanans. To take him from them would scar him. He's just a little boy, Sam."

"Damnit." He pounded his fist on the table. "This isn't fair."

Dallas nodded. "I agree with you. It's not fair. It's not fair to you, and it's ultimately not fair to Duke. He should be able to know his biological father if that father wants to be known. But right now he's a little boy, and if you take his mommy and daddy away from him, he'll be devastated."

Sam sighed heavily. Dallas was right. "What then? What are my options?"

"Your best option right now is to talk to Sydney. If she won't talk to you, talk to her parents. Most likely they're the legal parents and will make the decisions. Tell them you want to know the child, be a part of his life."

"They'll tell me to fuck off."

"What makes you say that?"

"They damn near already did."

"They were reacting, just as you were. They were scared you were going to take away the child they love."

"But—"

Dallas stopped him. "Trust me. If I felt there was the tiniest chance someone might take away one of my children, I'd react with all the anger in me to make sure it did not happen. That's how much a parent loves a child."

"I love him."

"You may. I don't know. But Sam, you didn't even know he existed yesterday. These two have raised him since he was an infant. They've fed him, housed him, clothed him, watched him grow. You represent a huge threat."

"I just want my son."

"You need to take yourself out of the equation right now. Yes, you were wronged. What Sydney did to you was wrong. But right now you have to think about the boy."

"Yes, I know." He pounded the table again. "Damnit."

Annie entered the kitchen. "Everything all right in here?"

"Yeah, Dr. Annie. I was just leaving." Sam stood.

"You don't have to go," Dallas said. "You want another drink?"

Sam looked down. He'd hardly touched his Scotch. He downed it and let the peaty alcohol burn his throat. Good stuff.

He thanked Dallas and Annie, told them he'd be touch, and drove back to his house near Zach and Dusty's.

Why hadn't Sydney told her parents he was the father?

He didn't know, but he was damn well going to find out.

CHAPTER NINE

Two days later, Sam still hadn't contacted Sydney or his son. He wasn't sure what the right course of action was. All he knew was that his heart had been broken, and he'd never let another woman in again.

What he would give to have his stale life back...

Why had he decided he needed to shake things up? Life in Montana was good. He was alone, but he wasn't lonely. He had his housekeeper and his hands, his dogs, cats, and livestock.

He'd missed his first bronc busting competition. His heart just wasn't in it. He no longer needed the cash. He was only doing it for fun.

Right now, Sam didn't really feel like having fun. He'd been doing ranch work for Zach, helping out where needed. Might as well get used to the place. He'd taken his meals alone in his little guest house, but he knew Dusty wouldn't put up with that much longer. If it weren't for the rodeo keeping her busy, she'd have rooted him out before now.

Speak of the devil. Dusty peeked through the window and a knock sounded on the door.

"Hey, stranger. Where've you been the last few days?"

"Just hangin' out."

"Why didn't you compete?"

"Didn't much feel like it."

"Oh." She didn't press it. *Thank God.* Then, "What's going on, Sam?"

He sighed. "I can't hide anything from you, can I?"

"Nope."

"Sit on down," he said. "It's a long story."

They sat together at the small table in the kitchen while Sam poured out the saga. After Dusty got over the shock, she gave him a hug.

"So Duke is Seanie's cousin."

"Pretty much."

"Why didn't Sydney tell you?"

"I have no clue. She didn't even tell her parents who the father was."

"Have you talked to them?"

"No. Not in a few days. I got some legal advice from Dallas, but I just haven't had the stamina to deal with it. It's going to be confrontational and ugly. It's not fair. I just want to see my son. To know him."

"I want you to come to dinner tonight."

"Why?"

"We're having a guest you need to talk to."

"Trust me, unless it's little Duke Buchanan, I'm not interested."

"Oh, I think you'll be interested in this person."

He sighed. "Who is it?"

"Thunder Morgan."

Ha. Any other time he'd jump at that chance, but not right now. "I'm not in the mood to discuss bronc busting, even with one of the greats."

"That's not why you need to talk to him."

"What the heck are you talking about, Dust?"

She winked. "Come to dinner and find out."

★ ★ ★

Sam had missed his first bronc busting event, and Sydney was worried.

How she missed him! Rod had been by twice, flashing more papers in her face about Duke and his birth and adoption. So now everyone knew. So what? It didn't matter. She'd already lost Sam. Her priority now was Duke. She had to protect him. He was a happy little boy, and she intended to make sure he stayed that way.

They'd spent a morning at the rodeo, eaten there, and Duke was exhausted and cranky. Carrie thought his forehead was slightly warm, so he was in his room with his mother now, napping. Roy sat across from Sydney at the table in her hotel room.

"Time to start talking, baby girl," Roy said. "I need to know why you wouldn't tell us who the father was. Sam O'Donovan is a good man from a good family. He would not have done wrong by you or Duke."

"It wasn't easy telling you the baby was a result of a one-night stand. No girl wants to tell her daddy that."

"No daddy wants to hear it, trust me. But at least now I know he was a good man. An upstanding man. Not some fly-by-night loser."

"You thought that?"

"Sydney, we didn't know what to think."

She sighed. "Yeah, I guess I can understand that."

"So start talking now, baby girl."

"Oh, Daddy." She took a drink of the iced tea in front of her. "It's not a long story or a particularly interesting one. It's actually really sad."

"I'm listening."

"How much do you know about the O'Donovans?"

"The girl married the middle McCray boy. They have a son. That's about it. We haven't been back here in a while. We certainly weren't welcome to visit Blake while he lived here."

"Yeah, I know."

"So what's the story?"

"I didn't know this at the time, of course. Sam and I did talk that first night, but not about anything really personal. Mostly about the rodeo and stuff. We seemed to have a lot in common, and I liked him a lot."

"So?"

"When I found out I was pregnant, I did some research on the O'Donovans."

"Yes?"

"I found out they had a sad history. Their daddy was a ranch hand for Jason McCray when they were little. Their mama died of leukemia when Sam was only ten. They moved to Montana to their grandparents' ranch so she could die there."

Roy nodded. "That *is* sad."

"It gets worse. When Dusty was eighteen, she got the same kind of leukemia. Her dad mortgaged the place to the hilt to pay for her treatment. Luckily she survived, and obviously she's fine now. But their dad committed suicide after nearly bankrupting their ranch. I didn't know till later that Dusty had married Zach McCray and she was fine. At the time, I thought Sam had to take care of her and the ranch. I just couldn't saddle him with another responsibility."

"But baby, that was not your choice to make."

"I knew enough about Sam to know he'd sacrifice everything to do the right thing, even if he didn't love me and didn't want a child. I thought I could spare him that. And I knew you and Mama had tried to have another child a few years before without any luck."

"How did you know that?"

"Mama told me."

"Yes, we did want another baby. Since we married so young, we were still young enough. But it didn't happen."

"I could make that happen for you. You've been great parents to Duke."

"He's a blessing, that's for sure. We won't give him up without a fight."

"I know that." She fiddled with strands of her hair. "I never thought I'd see Sam again. And I certainly never thought he'd find out about Duke."

"Sydney, you had to consider the possibility."

"He says he tried to look me up after that first night."

"It's not surprising that he didn't find you, especially if he didn't look too hard. You were on bed rest for a lot of the pregnancy and you got off the rodeo circuit for over a year after that."

"I know." She shook her head. "I had no idea he'd want to see me again. I mean, I figured it was just a one night thing for him."

"Was it that for you?"

She shook her head again. "No. Please believe me, Daddy, it was my first and last one-night stand."

"So you thought he was special, then?"

"Yes, I did, and I was right. He *is* special. And I've blown it for eternity."

"I won't sugar coat it, baby girl. You have made a mess of things. Not only for yourself and your mama and me, but mostly importantly for your innocent baby brother."

"I know. And I know we can't tell him what's going on. He won't understand."

"No, he won't."

"Oh, Daddy, what am I going to do?"

"I think you need to talk to Sam. Tell him the truth, exactly what you just told me."

"Will you come with me?"

Roy shook his head. "You're a grown-up, Sydney. You need to do this yourself. Clean up your own mess. Once we see how he reacts, I will certainly get involved, but for now, he deserves to hear the truth from you."

Sydney nodded. Her father was right, of course. "I will call him."

"No."

"No?"

"You will drive over to the McCray ranch and see him face-to-face, Sydney. That's the only way. He deserves that much."

"Okay."

There was only one problem.

Sam would not want to see her, let alone listen to her. But she'd cross that bridge when she got there. She looked around for her purse as her father opened the door to leave.

Standing in the doorway was Carrie, holding a listless Duke.

"Roy, there's something very wrong." Tears welled in her eyes. "He's burning up, and look at him! He's hardly moving."

"Now, Carrie, don't fret. He's probably just tired."

"Feel his forehead, damnit."

Sydney ran toward them while her father kissed the little

boy's forehead.

"Hmm, he is pretty hot," Roy said. "Did you bring a thermometer with you?"

"No, I didn't. I don't usually travel with one. My God, what kind of mother am I?"

"You're a great mother, Mama," Sydney said. "We'll just go on down to the pharmacy and get a thermometer and some children's ibuprofen, okay? He'll be fine."

"You two don't understand. This isn't a normal fever. He's had fevers before. A mother knows her child."

Sydney's heart jumped. *She* should be the one knowing when Duke was sick. She was his mother.

No. She was his sister. The woman holding him, crying over him, was his mother.

What was she going to do? If her parents lost Duke to Sam, they'd be devastated. It would be all her fault. Either her parents would hate her or Sam would.

No matter. Duke was the important thing right now.

"Okay, Mama. There's a doctor's office on Main Street. Let's just go on over there and see if he can take a look."

Carrie nodded. "I'd feel much better if we could have a doc look at him, Roy."

"All righty then, let's do it. Here, give him to me." Roy took the floppy little boy and the three of them drove the five blocks to Main Street.

They went in. "It's nearly six o'clock," the nurse said. "We're closing soon."

"Please," Carrie begged, "could he look at my son? He's burning up, and he's not acting right."

The nurse smiled. "Of course. Doc Larson never turns away a child in need. Wait here and I'll let him know you're here."

In a few moments, a bespectacled gray-haired man appeared. "Hello there. Bring the tyke on back and let's have a look."

"You stay here, Syd," Roy said.

"Please, let me," she begged. "He's—"

"All right. I understand." The three of them accompanied the doctor to an examining room.

"Hello, little fella," Doc said. "What's your name?"

"He's not very responsive," Carrie said.

"Can you tell the doc your name, son?" Roy asked.

"Duke," he said softly, his little boy treble stabbing Sydney's heart. How had she given up her baby?

"Duke, I'm going to have your daddy put you on the table here, okay?"

"'Kay."

Roy laid the little boy on the examining table, and Doc Larson inserted a thermometer in his ear. When it dinged, he looked at it and frowned.

"What?" Carrie asked frantically.

"Nearly 105. Is he prone to high fevers?"

"Not usually." Carrie's voice shook. "He usually never goes above 103, and that's only when he's really sick."

"Well, that alone isn't a huge worry," Doc said. "It's probably just a virus. I've seen some nasty ones going around. Let's get his shirt off and take a look and a listen."

Carrie pulled Duke's T-shirt over his head.

Doc put his stethoscope in his ears and placed the bell on Duke's chest. Then he turned. "How did he get this bruise?"

"What bruise?" Carrie asked.

"This one." Doc indicated a quarter-size bruise on Duke's

side.

"I'm not sure. We were at the rodeo all morning, till about two."

"How was he at the rodeo?"

"A little cranky. And he didn't seem to sleep well last night. Tossed and turned a lot."

"Can we get the rest of his clothes off? I want to take a look."

"Of course."

Duke whimpered as Carrie undressed him. Doc Larson took a look.

"Here's another bruise on his thigh, but I don't see any more. Has he fallen in the last day or so?"

"Not that I recall," Carrie said.

"Is he an unusually rowdy and rambunctious little boy?"

Roy wiped his forehead with a bandana. "He's a little boy, Doc. Of course he's rowdy and rambunctious. But he's been a little under the weather the past few days. We thought he was just catching a cold, but this fever's got us worried."

"Duke," Doc said, "see this bruise on your leg here?"

"Yeah."

"Can you remember how you got it? Did you fall down? Did something hit you in the leg?"

"I don't know."

"You can't remember anything that would have made you get a bruise?"

"No."

"It's okay, precious," Carrie said, rubbing his back. "So what do you think, Doc?"

Doc Larson's face was stern. "Honestly, it's probably nothing. As I said, there's some nasty crud going around right now. Viruses that cause fever and aches. I've seen a lot of kids with it. But Duke's fever is darned high."

"So what do we need to do?"

"I'm going to give him a little something to get the fever down, that's for sure, but I gotta say, I don't like those bruises."

"Little boys get bruises."

"You're traveling, though, and he's been in your sight at all times since you've been here, right?"

"Yes."

"Then you or he should know how he got those bruises."

"It's only two bruises," Carrie said, her voice still shaking.

Sydney's heart dropped to her belly.

Fever. Bruising.

Leukemia.

"I think we can let it go for twenty-four hours," Doc said. "I want to see him again tomorrow. The ibuprofen should get the fever down. Repeat the dosage every six hours. Keep liquids in him and make sure he gets lots of rest."

"Doc?" Sydney stepped forward.

"Yes, young lady?"

"I think you should know something."

"Of course. What is it?"

"Both his paternal grandmother and aunt had—oh God— leukemia."

Carrie's hands whipped to her mouth. "Sydney, what are you talking about?"

Doc Larson's expression went grave.

"Carrie, take Duke out of here," Roy said.

"Roy—"

"Just do it, please. I'll explain everything as soon as I can."

Carrie dressed Duke quickly and left the room.

"Doc, Duke is not my wife's and my biological child. He's our grandchild. May I speak confidentially?"

"Absolutely," Doc said.

"Sydney is his mother, and the father is a man named Sam O'Donovan."

"Sam? I know his sister, Dusty, well." Doc's face went white. "Dear Lord."

"That's why I told you," Sydney said. "I'm so afraid."

Doc scribbled some notes on a pad and handed it to Roy. "Take the boy to Denver. He needs some blood work pronto."

"Okay, Doc. We'll take him first thing in the morning."

Doc's eyes softened as he touched Roy's arm. "Take him now."

CHAPTER TEN

The dinner at Dusty's with Thunder Morgan had been pleasant. He regaled them with tales of his bronc busting days, and Sam smiled and laughed, almost forgetting about Sydney and Duke.

But not quite.

Now they sat in the family room, having an after dinner drink.

"Thunder," Dusty said, "would you mind telling Sam a little about you and Amber?"

Sam jerked his head. Amber was Thunder's daughter, right? Why would Dusty think he needed to know anything about that?

"Not at all," the man said. "What would you like to know?"

The woman was about to be married to Harper Bay. Surely Thunder couldn't think Sam was interested in her. What the hell was Dusty doing?

"I'm not sure what I want to know myself," Sam said. "What are you getting at, Dust?"

"It's common news around here, and neither Thunder nor Amber mind talking about it. I thought their circumstances might interest you."

"Uh, well—" Sam didn't want to be rude, but he couldn't imagine why he'd be interested in their "circumstances."

"Sam has had an issue come up in his life, and I think he'd benefit by hearing about you and Amber."

"All right." Thunder cleared his throat. "I only met my beautiful daughter a little over two months ago."

Sam jerked forward. "What?"

"Yup, it's the truth. I had one night with her mother twenty-some years ago. I never even knew Amber existed till I met her."

"And you're sure she's yours?"

"Absolutely." He nodded. "I recalled her mother. And Amber, though she looks an awful lot like Karen, definitely has my eyes. That was all the proof I needed."

"Really?"

"Yes. But Amber wanted to be sure. She didn't want to force herself on me. Heck, she wasn't forcin' herself. I was glad to have her. Never did have a family of my own. But it was important to her, so we had a DNA test."

"And she's definitely yours?"

"Yep. Definitely. I couldn't be happier or more proud to have her in my life."

"Wow." Not only was Thunder Morgan his all-time idol, but they had more than bronc busting in common.

"Dusty," Zach interjected, "maybe we should let these two talk."

"Oh, it's okay," Sam said. "I don't mind if you're here. I assume Dusty told you everything anyway, right?"

"Yes," Zach said, "and I know you don't have any secrets from your sister, but let's give them a little privacy, okay, Dusty?"

She nodded. "We can go read Seanie a story."

They left the spacious family room, leaving Sam alone with Thunder Morgan.

"So," Thunder said, "I take it there's a reason why your

baby sis wanted you to know about Amber and me."

"Yeah, there is." Sam cleared his throat. "I'm kind of in a similar situation right now."

"Well, son, don't just sit there stuttering. Tell me what's going on."

He poured out the story of Sydney and Duke.

"In a way, you're luckier than I was," Thunder said. "You know about your boy now. I missed twenty-two years of my baby girl's life, a life I could have helped make a lot better. She had some rough times."

"What's your relationship with Amber's mother?"

"Well, that's kind of a sad thing. Karen—that's her name—isn't well. She's in rehab for alcoholism right now, and she's also gettin' psychotherapy and medication. She's been diagnosed with bipolar disorder and borderline personality disorder.

"Oh, wow. I'm sorry to hear that."

"Amber didn't have it easy, growin' up with Karen. I feel a lot of guilt about not being there for her. Or for Karen, for that matter."

"But did you even know you had a daughter?"

He shook his head. "No, I didn't. Evidently Karen tried to contact me after Amber was born, but I never got the message. I was livin' with a woman at the time who told Karen never to call me again. The woman was obsessed with me. I later got a restraining order against her."

"Wow." Sam shook his head. "But you shouldn't feel guilty. You didn't even know she existed."

"Doesn't matter. She's mine. I could have made her life easier."

"Does she blame you?"

"No, absolutely not. She understands. She's a wonderful

young woman."

"Then you shouldn't blame yourself."

Thunder nodded. "Objectively I know that. But it's easier said than done."

The ache in Sam's heart eased a little. But only a little. "At least I know my boy has had a good life so far."

"That's something to be said, for sure," Thunder agreed.

"But I can't help but be really angry," Sam said. "I wasn't even given a choice to be a part of his life."

"Nor was I."

"I know, I know. And you missed a lot more than I did. Don't you resent Amber's mother for not telling you?"

"Like I said, she tried to tell me once. The woman scared her enough to never try again. And Karen's illness helped her keep that promise. She was paranoid."

"I'm sorry you missed so much."

"So am I. I feel a lot of guilt over Amber's tough life. But she sets me straight. She's so loving and giving. I wish I had been there for her when she needed me, but I'm here now, and right now, the best thing I can do for Amber is see that her mother gets the help she needs."

"You're a very forgiving man."

"Nah, there's nothin' special about me. But when you get to a certain age, you realize that resentment only breeds more resentment. So I've chosen to focus on now. Amber still needs a father—maybe not the same way she did when she was a little girl, but she needs me. And I sure as heck need her."

"What should I do? My son is only five. If I uproot him, he will suffer."

"That's a tough one, for sure," Thunder said. "I wish I had an answer for you."

Sam stood and paced in a circle. "I'm so angry."

"I can't tell you what to do about your son. My situation is totally different. Amber's an adult and can make her own decisions. But I can give you this advice. Let the anger go, Sam. If you truly want a relationship with your boy, the anger will only hold you back."

Sam walked to the bar and refreshed his drink. "You need some more?" He held up the bottle of Scotch.

"Nope, I'm good for now."

"I just wish I knew what to do."

"Do you care for the child's mother?"

Sam took a stiff belt of the Scotch. "I thought I did."

"And now?"

"Now I don't know. Sydney's amazing, but she's lied to me twice now."

"Twice?"

"When I ran into her again at the rodeo a few days ago, we hooked up. After that, I learned she was engaged."

"Oh, Jesus."

"Yeah. He showed up while I was still in her room. She broke up with him and later told me she'd been planning to end it anyway, but still, it was dishonest."

"Yes, it was."

"But that was nothing compared to this. She's kept my son from me for five years."

"She may have had a reason. Have you asked her?"

"She can't possibly have any reason that would make any sense."

"She obviously didn't keep the child. She let her mother and father adopt him."

"Yeah. They legally adopted him. Dallas McCray looked

into it. He called this morning with that piece of news. It might have been easier for me if they were just raising him and he was still legally Sydney's child. It'd be easier for me to assert my parental rights in that case."

"But now he has a legal mother and father who love him."

"Yes, and more importantly, who *he* loves. What kind of horrid man would I be to take a baby away from his mom and dad?"

"I wouldn't call you horrid."

"I feel like one big asshole. But I want my child, Thunder." He sat down and cupped his head in his hands. "I just don't know what to do."

"And as for Sydney?"

Sydney. What a mess. "A couple days ago I thought I was in love with her."

"Love? In this short time?"

"Yes, damnit. I know it sounds ridiculous, but I've never dated anyone who makes me feel the way she does. Or did. Or does. Aw hell, I don't know what the fuck I'm saying."

"Son, I'm going to give you some advice, and it's up to you whether you take it."

"All right. I'm listenin'." Why not? He sure as hell didn't know what to do. Maybe Thunder had some answers.

"I gave my life to the rodeo. Hell, I had my one nighters—that's what Amber's mother was. I'm not proud of it, but I was a young cowboy and women liked me. My life was on the road. I traveled all over and won purse after purse. I had a good life, had all I wanted, but it got mighty lonely comin' home every night."

"Are you saying you have regrets?"

"Would I do it differently if I could?" He shook his head.

"I don't know. Knowin' what I do now, yes, I think I would. I retired a few years ago, as you know, and I was livin' alone on a ranch on the western slope. Life was good. Peaceful. But I can't tell you what a glow Amber has brought to my life. I'm giving her away at her wedding Saturday, did you know that? I've only been her father for two months and she's lettin' me have that honor."

Sam nodded.

Thunder continued, "People, son. Family. Those are the precious things in life. If you think you love this woman, this woman who gave birth to your child, you owe it to yourself to give it the shot it deserves."

"What if it doesn't work?"

"There are no guarantees in life. You know that better than anyone, being a bronc buster. There's no guarantee you aren't gonna bust a rib or worse when that stud bucks you off."

Sam nodded. The man was right.

"So my advice to you is to go get her."

What about Duke? Sam opened his mouth to say as much, when Dusty came rushing in.

"Sam!"

"What is it?"

"Sydney just called." Her eyes filled with tears. "They've taken Duke to Denver to the hospital." She doubled over, her breath coming in rapid puffs.

"Take it easy, darlin'," Zach said, helping her to the couch.

"What, Dusty? What's wrong with Duke?"

Zach looked up, his eyes sober. "They think he might have leukemia."

CHAPTER ELEVEN

Sam drove to Denver at top speed. When he reached the hospital, he parked quickly and ran inside.

Roy was waiting in the emergency room waiting area. "Carrie and Syd are in with him. His fever's come down quite a bit, thank God, and he's much livelier now."

"That's a good sign, right?" Sam said.

Roy shook his head. "Hell, I don't know. I wish I knew what was going on. My little boy has a fever and some bruises, and all of a sudden we're talking about the C word? I can't deal with this. Four days ago I didn't know who his biological father was, and now I find out leukemia runs in the family."

"Leukemia isn't usually hereditary," Sam said. "At least that's what they've always told us. It was just bad luck that both Ma and Dusty got the same disease."

"Yes, the doctors here have assured us of the same thing. Still, Doc Larson seemed very adamant that we bring Duke in tonight once he found out about your mother and your sister."

"Doc Larson's a small-town doctor. He's a good man, but he probably isn't up to date on his research. Plus, leukemia is highly curable."

"But your mother..."

"She didn't make it." Sam gulped. "But that was a long time ago. Treatment is better now. And look at Dusty. She's healthy as a horse."

Carrie came out white-faced. "They've drawn all the

blood. It's going to take a few hours to get the results. Hello, Sam."

Sam stood. "How is he?"

"He's better." Her face was streaked from tears. "Sydney is sitting with him now."

"May I see him?"

"He doesn't even know you," Carrie said.

"Carrie," Roy said, his voice soft yet stern. "He needs to see the child. Try to understand."

Carrie nodded. "Go on in."

Sam walked into the room and the sound of childish laughter was like a symphonic concerto to his ears. Duke was laughing. Sydney, her face swollen and puffy, her brooding dark eyes sunken, smiled at the little boy. *SpongeBob SquarePants* played on the television.

"Hello," Sam said.

Sydney looked up, startled. "Sam." She wiped her nose. "Hello."

"How's the little fella doing?"

"He's actually doing better. We're just waiting now."

"Your mom told me."

"Who's that, Sassy?" the little boy asked.

"Sweetie, this is a good friend of mine," Sydney said. "His name is Sam."

Sam smiled and walked forward, holding out his hand. To his surprise, the boy took it, shaking like a man.

"I hear you've been a little under the weather," Sam said.

"Yeah. They poked me and took blood out of me."

"Well, that didn't bother a big boy like you, did it?"

"Nah. Mama and Sassy cried, but I didn't."

Sam ruffled Duke's hair—hair so like his own. "So what's

on the tube?"

"Duke's favorite," Sydney said. "SpongeBob."

They watched television for a few minutes, saying nothing, until Roy and Carrie came back into the room. "Sydney," Roy said, "you take a break for a while. Mom and I will stay with Duke."

Sydney nodded and stood up. She glanced at Sam. Was he supposed to go with her?

Fine.

"Good to meet you, Duke," he said. "I'll be back to check on you later, okay?"

"Okay." The boy smiled.

Sam's heart melted. His son was a beautiful child. He had to be okay. He just had to be.

Sam wasn't sure what to say, how to act around Sydney. One look at her and he knew he loved her. Feelings didn't turn on and off like a water faucet. No sirree. And something else was evident as well. This woman loved her son—her brother—however she thought of him.

This was killing her. As much as it was killing him.

"You want some coffee?" he asked.

She nodded. "Sure."

"Go on and sit down in the waiting area. I'll go get it."

Sydney took his arm. "No. I'll come along with you if you don't mind. I just can't sit anymore. I feel like I'm just sitting around waiting for bad news. I hate it."

Sam nodded. His gut clenched and he felt helpless, as he'd felt so many times before in similar situations. He knew how Sydney was feeling. He'd done his share of waiting around with Dusty for results. It was damned hard.

They walked out of the ER and through a walkway that

led to the regular hospital. That area was quiet. It was late, and visiting hours were over. Sam scoped out the coffee shop.

"Damn. It's closed."

Sydney let out a huff of air. "Just my luck." She leaned against a wall next to a supply closet. "Sam?"

"What?"

"Would you please hold me?"

He wanted to hold her until the end of time, but what good would it do?

God, I love her. Love her with all my heart. But he could never be with her.

Yet she was still the mother of his child, and she needed comfort.

He took her in his arms and held her body close.

She was tall, nearly six feet, he guessed, and fit perfectly against his own six-feet-three-inch frame. Her ample breasts pressed against his chest. How good it felt to hold the woman he loved.

The woman he loved and could never have.

She let out a sniff. "I'm so scared, Sam."

"I know, sweetheart. I'm scared too."

"How are we supposed to get through this?"

He shook his head. "I don't know. You just do, I guess. I remember waiting around with Dusty for blood tests. Wanting to do something but knowing I couldn't do anything. Wishing it were me instead of her. It's horrible."

"That's just how it is."

"I know, and I'm sorry you have to go through it."

She lifted her head and gazed at him, her dark eyes sunken and sad. "You really do know."

"Yes."

"You poor thing. God, you poor thing!"

"It's okay."

"No, it's not even close to okay. I'm so sorry, Sam. I'm so sorry for everything."

"Don't worry about that now. Let's focus on Duke."

She nodded, and then, out of nowhere, she wrapped her arms around his neck and pulled him into a kiss.

Her lips smashed to his with a force so raw, he wasn't sure he'd experienced anything like it. She trailed her tongue across the seam of his lips, looking for entrance. He granted it, and her mouth had never tasted sweeter. Their tongues met and dueled, tangled together in a kiss of passion, of desire, an expression of life.

Sam backed her up against the wall and pushed into her, his erection straining against his jeans.

She met him eagerly, pushing into his hardness, spreading her legs so that his thigh was between them. She begin to writhe against his jean-clad thigh, rubbing herself.

What a turn-on! But how could he be turned on right now, when so much else demanded his attention?

Yet it made perfect sense. Here they were, loving each other, validating their lives.

He forced his thigh upward and she groaned. He rubbed it against her vulva, matching the thrust of his tongue in her mouth.

He had to have her. Had to have her now. Right here in the hospital hallway. He didn't care who walked by, who might be in the next room.

Room.

The supply closet.

He jiggled the doorknob and it opened.

"In here, baby," he said.

The small room was dark and smelled of pine, but he didn't care, nor did Sydney seem to. He unzipped her jeans and thrust his fingers into her heat.

Soaking wet for him. He thought he might cream for her right there.

"Sam, Sam, I need you," she whimpered into his shoulder.

"It's dark in here, sweetheart. Take off your boots and jeans. I'd do it for you but I can't see."

Fabric rustled. He fumbled with his own belt and jeans and pushed them down to his knees. When she came toward him, he lifted her and placed her on his rigid cock.

"Oh God." She sighed.

"Yeah, baby. God, you have no idea how much I need this."

"I have a pretty good idea," she said.

She clung to him, and he held onto her with his strong arms and moved her up and down upon his hardness.

Her sleek warmth gloved him like no other. If only this could last forever. If only.

He wanted her to come, but he couldn't let go of her to touch her clit. As if reading his mind, she snaked one arm between their bodies and began to stimulate herself.

And he was even more turned on than before.

He lifted her soft body up, to the tip of his cock, and lowered her down to his base.

Sweet sensation.

Sweet fuck.

No.

Sweet love.

This wasn't a fuck. This was making love.

He was making love to his woman in a hospital supply

closet, but it didn't matter. It was love, pure and simple, and it was a validation of the life that flowed through their veins.

"Sam, I'm coming. I'm coming!"

Sydney's warmth throbbed against him, and he let himself go.

The convulsions started at the base of his cock and shot through as he shot into her. His veins pulsed, his muscles contracted. His whole body went rigid, relaxed, and went rigid again. When he wasn't sure he could stand any longer, he had to let Sydney go.

"I'm sorry, baby. I have to put you down."

Her legs slid down his thighs. "It's okay. God, it's okay. That was amazing."

"Yes, it was." *God, it was.*

"You are amazing, Sam. It's you. It's not the act. It's you."

He wanted to say the words back to her because he meant them with all his heart. How could he live without her?

Could he forgive her?

What about Duke?

Duke.

His baby son might be very ill right now. How had he gotten so out of control that he was fucking in a closet when his son might be gravely ill?

"Jesus," he said. "What the fuck are we doing?"

His eyes had adjusted to the dark. Sydney was pulling on her boots. "Making love, I think."

"Sydney, our son is in the hospital. We have no right to be acting so foolishly. What were we thinking?"

She sighed. "I was thinking I wanted to be in your arms. Is that so wrong?"

"When our son is lying in a hospital bed and when we

have many issues to work out between us—some of which I don't think can ever be worked out—yes, it's wrong. It's selfish and wrong."

"I didn't see you stopping me."

He sighed. She was right, of course. He should have kept his head—the one *above* his shoulders. "Well, I'm stopping you now."

"Now? What good does that do? What's done is done. You got your rocks off just like I did. Admit it, you wanted it as much as I did."

Of course he did. But damned if he'd admit anything to her.

He pulled his pants up and buckled his belt. "We'd better hit the restroom before we go back to the ER. To make sure we look okay."

"I already look like shit. I've been crying and worrying for the last several hours. My parents will understand that."

She was right again. "Fine. Let's just get back there. Now."

They walked back in silence and sat down in the waiting area of the ER.

Within five minutes, Roy came out to find them.

"You two come on back now," he said. "The doc's on his way with the results."

CHAPTER TWELVE

Sydney's heart dropped to her stomach. She gulped. *Please, please let him be okay. I'll do anything. I'll give up anything. Anything as long as he's okay.*

The doctor entered with Duke's chart.

"Mr. and Mrs. Buchanan," he said.

"Please don't beat around the bush," Carrie begged. "What's going on with our little boy?"

Duke had fallen asleep in the bed and appeared comfortable.

"I'm not going to beat around the bush. The news is good. Duke's blood counts came back in the normal range."

Sydney fell into Sam's hard body.

"And that means?" Roy said.

"It means Duke has a virus. He'll be good as new in a few days. Keep him rested and push fluids. Give him ibuprofen for the fever as needed."

"But the bruises," Carrie said.

"He's a little boy. Little boys get bruises. It's not uncommon for a little boy to not know how he got a bruise."

"But Doc Larson—"

"Doc Larson did the right thing by telling you to come here, especially with the medical history. Although as I said before, blood cancers are rarely hereditary. I'd like you to repeat the blood work in a month, just to make sure. I'll write out the instructions for your pediatrician at home."

"Thank you," Carrie breathed. "Thank you so much!"

Sydney burst into tears.

"He's okay, sweetheart," Sam said. "He's okay."

"I know that. It's just... I don't know."

"You're letting down," the doctor said. "Completely understandable and normal. I'm so sorry you had this scare. But Duke is just fine."

"Should we get him home to Nevada right away?" Carrie asked.

"There's no reason why you can't continue your visit," the doctor said. "It's really up to you. He'd be more comfortable at home, of course, but the travel might be difficult for him. If you stay, he'll be on the mend by the time you leave, and the trip will be much more comfortable for him."

"I have another barrel race the day after tomorrow," Sydney said, "but I'd feel better if you and Daddy took Duke home."

"Well, we can't go anywhere tonight," Roy said. "Let's get him back to Bakersville to the hotel and make sure he gets a good night's sleep. We can make that decision in the morning." He held out his hand. "Thank you so much, Doctor."

"You're most welcome." He handed Roy a paper. "Here's the instructions for your pediatrician. You all have a good night."

Carrie picked up a sleeping Duke.

"Just a minute, Doctor," Sam said.

"Yes?"

"I assume you still have Duke's blood sample?"

"Of course. It's in the lab."

"Then I want you draw some of mine. I want a DNA test."

"Excuse me? I'm not sure I understand."

"He's my son. I want proof."

Sydney's stomach tumbled. "Please, Sam, not right now."

"Right now's the perfect time. He's already had his blood drawn so we don't have to poke him again. And he's sleeping. He can't hear us."

"I can't run another test without parental consent." He turned to Roy and Carrie. "Are you okay with this?"

"No," Carrie said. "I am not."

Roy soothed her. "Carrie, it will happen sooner or later. If we do it now it saves Duke an additional pinprick."

"You realize insurance won't cover this," the doctor said.

"I can pay you cash money right now," Sam said. "Or put it on a credit card. I don't give a damn what it costs."

"All right. We're not in the habit of drawing blood for paternity tests in the ER, but since you're here, I can arrange it. You come with me." He nodded to Sam. "I'll send a nurse in with paperwork for you to sign," he said to Roy and Carrie.

Sydney plunked down in a chair, feeling utterly defeated. "I'm sorry," she said to her parents.

"What are we going to do?" Carrie sobbed.

"Look," Roy said, "the most important thing is that Duke is okay. Our little boy does not have leukemia. Grasp that concept, and everything else is nothing."

"Everything else is *not* nothing," Carrie said. "That man wants to take our son."

"Lower your voice." Roy put his fingers against his lips. "Do you want to wake him? Now just settle down. We have to accept that Sam is going to be a part of Duke's life. There's nothing we can do. He's the child's father."

Sydney sat, numb and silent.

A nurse entered. "Here are the papers for you to sign."

Roy scribbled his signature.

"I can't believe you're letting him do this," Carrie said.

"If we don't, he'll just get a court order. Duke's blood has already been drawn."

"There's no need," Sydney said. "Only one man can be the father, and it's Sam. You can trust me on that."

"He needs to know for sure, and I don't blame him."

"But this will only help him," Carrie said. "It will give him the ammunition he needs to take Duke away from us."

"No one is taking Duke away from us. You can count on that," Roy said. "Now simmer down."

Sam returned, a Band-Aid in the crease of his elbow. "I'll get the results in a few days."

"I hope you're happy," Carrie said.

"As a matter of fact, I am," Sam said. "I'm happy that Duke is not seriously ill. I've had enough catastrophic illness affecting people I love to last a lifetime. I really didn't want to go through that again."

Carrie lowered her gaze, and Sydney felt bad for her mother. Sam had shamed her a little.

"Do you mind if I ride back with Sam?" Sydney asked. "We need to talk."

Her father understood. She could tell by the expression on his face. "Yes, that's fine, baby girl."

"Well, I don't know—" Sam began.

"Please, Sam. Just give me the ride to Bakersville. It's only an hour or so."

Sam sighed. "All right. We can stop and grab a bite on the way. Suddenly I'm famished."

Sydney's tummy tightened. She wasn't famished. Not hungry at all. Gratitude filled her for her little boy's health, but still so much remained unresolved.

Maybe the drive home with Sam would resolve some of it. She hoped, at least.

★ ★ ★

"So you expect me to believe that you didn't tell your parents who the father was because you didn't want to lay a child on me? With all my other problems?"

Sydney gulped. She'd never expected him to question her reasons why. They were the truth, after all. "I was young. Those were my thoughts at the time."

"Unbelievable."

"Plus, you hardly knew me. It was a one-night stand. Did you really want me coming to you with news of a baby?"

"I don't know, Sydney. I'll never know how I would have felt, because you didn't let me have the chance to feel anything, did you?"

He was right. What could she say? Except, "I'm sorry, Sam. I'm so sorry."

"Doesn't cut it."

"I know that. But I am sorry. Truly."

"You know, I could almost understand if you'd had the baby and then put him up for adoption. I'd still be upset, but I could at least understand. You weren't ready for a baby. You didn't think I'd want him either. Course you'd have been wrong about that, but I can at least see the reasoning. But that's not what you did. You had the baby, didn't tell me, and gave him to your parents to raise."

"They wanted another child. My mama was only seventeen when Blake was born, twenty when I came along.

She was only thirty-nine when Duke was born. She and Dad had tried to have another child for several years, but it didn't happen. Duke was a godsend for them."

"Maybe he would have been a godsend to me. Did you think of that?"

"No. I didn't, and I'm sorry. I thought it was a one-night stand and you wouldn't want the baby."

"You were wrong."

"I realize that now." Memory washed over her of that incredible night together, the night that had resulted in their beautiful son. How could she make him understand when she wasn't sure she understood herself?

"You got the best of both worlds, didn't you? You got the baby without the responsibility. Instead of being the responsible parent, you get to be the doting big sister."

Guilt rolled through her like hot lava. It was true. She couldn't deny that she liked being a part of Duke's life. Giving him away to strangers would have been too hard. But she couldn't say these words to Sam.

Didn't matter. He already knew anyway.

They drove the rest of the way in silence, until Sydney noticed they'd passed through town and were into ranching country.

"Where are we going?"

"Aw, fuck," Sam said. "I was on autopilot. We're heading to Dusty and Zach's ranch. Shit, now I have to turn around. We're almost there, too."

"No matter. You're exhausted and so am I. Are you staying at a guest house?"

"Yeah."

"Is there more than one bedroom?"

"Yeah."

"Just keep going then. I'll sleep in the other bedroom."

"Look, it's no problem to go back."

"Sam, please. We've both been through the wringer tonight. Let's just go to bed."

He relented and kept driving.

★ ★ ★

Sydney woke in the darkness. A warm body had snuggled against her back, spoon fashion. She jerked.

"It's just me, baby," Sam said. "Go back to sleep."

She smiled and curled against him.

When she opened her eyes to dawn streaming through the window, he was gone.

The smoky aroma of bacon wafted into her room. She rose and pulled on her jeans and shirt and traipsed out to the kitchen.

Sam stood at the stove in jeans, shirtless, his bronze muscular back a sight to behold. Had a more beautiful man ever been made?

"Good morning," she said.

He turned. "Morning. Coffee's made. Help yourself."

Was that it? Was he going to say nothing about the fact that he'd slept against her last night?

"Uh, okay. Thanks."

She fumbled in the cupboards until she found a mug and poured herself a cup.

"Like scrambled eggs?" he asked.

"Love 'em."

"Good. They'll be ready in a minute or two."

So this was how it was going to be. *Fine. I get it.*

He set a plate of eggs in front of her, and the doorbell rang. "Excuse me for a minute."

In walked Dallas McCray, the oldest of the McCray brothers. Sydney remembered him.

"Sydney, this is Dusty's brother-in-law Dallas," Sam said.

"We've met. Nice to see you."

"You too," Dallas said. He turned to Sam. "You want me to come back later?"

"No. This concerns her. Sit on down. I'll get you some coffee."

What on earth was going on?

"Dallas is an attorney," Sam said.

"I'm a rancher with a license to practice law," Dallas said. "I don't claim to know everything about the law."

"You know enough for me," Sam said. "What did you find out?"

"To proceed with anything, you'll need to get a DNA test."

"Already done."

"What?"

"The DNA test. Got it yesterday. I'll have the results in a few days."

"How'd you manage that? I thought we'd need a court order."

"Circumstances. I was in the right place at the right time."

Sydney widened her eyes. "I can't believe this. What the hell is going on?"

"I'm going after my rights, Sydney."

"Meaning?"

"I want my son."

"You can't possibly be serious. You're not taking him away

from my parents. I won't let you."

"You gave away your parental rights. I did not."

"And you agree with this?" she said to Dallas.

"I'm just the lawyer here. It's not my job to agree or disagree. It's my job to answer his questions about the law, and that's what I'm doing. He already knows I can't represent him in any kind of legal action. I have a ranch to run."

"Then who's representing him?"

"A friend of mine in Denver. Richard White. He's a family lawyer. He specializes in this kind of stuff."

"How much is this costing you?" she asked Sam.

"Don't righteously care," he said. "Hang the cost. I want my kid."

"Don't put the cart before the horse," Dallas said. "We can't do anything until we get the DNA results."

"I can guarantee what the results will be. And so can you, can't you, Sydney?"

Her cheeks warmed. "He's the father," she said. "I haven't been with anyone else." She turned to Sam. "After everything we went through last night, I can't believe you still want to do this."

"Last night only clinched it," he said. "Last night proved how fragile life is. I'm glad as hell Duke isn't sick, but damnit, anything can happen. Last night drove home that you never know what tomorrow may bring. I want to know my son now, because only God knows how much more time he and I have together."

Sydney opened her mouth to speak but shut it quickly. What could she say to that? He made a damn good point.

"Tell me," Sam said to her. "If you were in my place, what would you do? Say you had a kid out there you just found out about. Wouldn't you want to get to know him?'

"I...I don't know. The situation is completely different. I'm a woman. If I had a kid out there, I'd know it."

"I think you just made my point. You can't even begin to understand how I feel, can you? Women think they can make all the decisions because they have the babies. Well, I'll grant you the fact that it's your body. If you had decided to abort the baby, I wouldn't have had any say in it."

Sydney gasped. "I could never have done that."

"I'm not saying you could have." Sam's tone softened a bit. "I'm just saying it was your decision. But that baby is half mine, and the minute he came out of your body, he stopped being solely your business."

"Fathers do have rights," Dallas said.

Sydney pounded her fist on the table. "I understand all that."

"Then what's the problem?" Sam said, still softly. "I'm just asserting my rights."

"Can't you at least talk to my parents? Maybe we can all work something out."

"That's an option you haven't considered, Sam," Dallas said, "and it's something that makes real sense from where I see it. Remember, the court will consider what's in the best interest of the child, not the parent. You can love that boy all you want, and you can want to be with him and raise him all you want, but if the court thinks leaving him with the Buchanans is in his best interest, that's what they'll do."

Sam raked his fingers through his hair. The taut muscles in his forearm tightened. *Good. Dallas had made him think.*

"Without the court involved, I have no way of knowing they'd keep any agreement we made between us."

"My parents are good people," Sydney said. "They would keep their word."

"And just how do I know that? I don't know your parents. How do I know they're trustworthy?"

After all, their daughter sure isn't. A knife sliced into Sydney's heart as she heard the words Sam didn't say.

And it was the truth. She hadn't been very trustworthy. She hadn't told him about Rod. And way more importantly, she hadn't told him about Duke.

Dallas took a sip of his coffee. "This is clearly getting personal between the two of you. I think I should leave." He stood.

"You don't have to go," Sam said.

"Yes, I do," Dallas said. "You two need to come to some kind of understanding. If you don't want to do it for yourselves, do it for Duke." He left.

"Damnit, Sydney!" Sam gripped the edge of the table with both hands.

"What?"

His eyes blazed. "It's not a crime to want to be a part of my son's life. Why can't anyone understand that?"

"It's not that we don't understand..."

"What then? What is it?"

She tried to smile. Didn't quite make it. "We just all love him so much."

Sam seemed to soften a little. "I know that." He sighed. "I really do know that, Sydney."

Reality hit her. He did understand. Just like she understood how he was feeling, how he wanted to be a part of Duke's life. If only she had handled the situation differently from the beginning. Then he wouldn't think her untrustworthy now.

She reached forward and covered one of Sam's hands with her own. His brown gaze shifted to hers

"I'm so sorry," she said, "about all of this."

He nodded. "Yeah, me too." He ungripped the table, moved toward her, and helped her to her feet. "Sydney." His voice was rough as it cracked.

"Yes?"

"Will you come to bed with me?

She nodded.

CHAPTER THIRTEEN

He picked her up and carried her to the other bedroom, presumably his, and tossed her on the bed. Fire burned in his eyes. He was going to be rough.

But she was ready for it. She wanted him to take her. Make her his.

He ripped off her clothes quickly and with a vengeance, until she lay nude upon the bed. Sam, still fully clothed, rose and went to the dresser. He returned with two red bandanas.

"Grab the headboard," he said.

Sydney jerked. "What?"

"Did I stutter? Grab two of the bars on the headboard. Make sure you're comfortable. You'll be in this position for a little while."

The bandanas. *Oh God, he's going to tie my wrists to the headboard.* Fear rushed through her, accompanied by a strange arousal.

"Sam, I don't think—"

"I don't recall asking what you thought. If you don't want to do this, you can leave."

"You mean I'm free to go?"

"Of course you're free to go. I'd never keep you against your will. What kind of man do you think I am?"

Up until now, she thought she'd known. She'd never imagined him tying her up. Had he been a calf roper? She couldn't remember.

I should go. I should run like the wind out of here. But a force like the strongest magnet kept her supine on the bed.

"So you're staying?"

She nodded. She most likely needed her head examined, but she was staying.

"Good." His voice was husky, stern.

He would not hurt her. She trusted him.

She understood now. He didn't think she was trustworthy. He would prove to her that *he* was.

He regarded her, his eyes blazing. He sat down next to her and blindfolded her with one of the bandanas.

She was not expecting that. She thought he'd use them to tie her wrists to the headboard.

The cotton fabric brushed against her skin as he tied first one and then the other wrist to the headboard.

His lips brushed her ear. "Do you trust me?" he whispered.

Warmth flooded her veins. "Yes. I trust you, Sam."

"Good." He tightened the fabric around both wrists.

Her body burned. Electricity crackled between them and her veins popped with energy. Excitement overwhelmed her. She was scared, her nerves hopped within her skin, but she was turned on. Oh, so turned on.

She lay still for several minutes, wondering what he was up to. When she thought she could stand it no longer, coldness touched one nipple.

Ice. He was rubbing an ice cube over her nipple.

"Relax, baby," he said softly. "I won't hurt you."

She nodded. "I know."

"Enjoy the sensations."

She breathed in, breathed out, willed her body to relax.

The ice on her nipple melted, and droplets of water

tickled the flesh of her breasts as they oozed downward. The ice touched her other nipple, and this time the sensation wasn't so abrupt. It was cold and harsh, yet her nipple hardened and strained upward. She wanted the warmth of his lips to soothe the cold.

But his lips didn't come. Only the ice melting and drizzling down her breast like the frosting on a hot cinnamon roll.

With both nipples cold and hard, the ice disappeared.

"Oh!"

It had reappeared within in seconds...on her clit.

"Easy, sweetheart," he soothed. "Hold still."

Her knees buckled.

"I said hold still." His voice was stern this time. It left no question that he meant to be obeyed.

She obeyed.

Images of him tying her feet to the foot of the bed swirled through her mind. And her nipples hardened even further at that thought.

The ice cube smoothed back and forth over the folds of her flesh.

"Mmm, it's melting fast. You're so hot down here."

Again, the icy coldness made her long for the heat of his lips, his mouth.

Again, they didn't come.

She needed to be touched by a human hand, mouth, lips. No more ice. She wanted human contact. Sam contact.

The ice melted into oblivion, and then...ah, yes. His tongue found her. Finally.

He flicked it over her hard bud and she wrapped her legs around his muscular back. His skin was warm and smooth, and though she couldn't see, she knew it was glowing and beautiful.

"Sam, yes, yes." Her voice seemed to come from without her. Funny how taking away her vision made her voice seem distant. He continued licking, and then fingers closed around each of her nipples. He was playing with them while he pleasured her.

Holy Christ, it felt good. Not knowing what he'd do next was oddly exciting. Oddly arousing.

His tongue darted in and out of her wetness. When he clamped his lips around her clit, an orgasm burst through her.

Crazy bursts, like fireworks. No build up this time. She was coming, just coming, out of nowhere. And God, it was good.

"Yeah, baby, come for me." His fingers continued to work her nipples as he soothed her clit with his tongue after her climax. "Come for me again."

And as though he demanded her obedience with mere words, she burst into flames once more.

Once more he brought her to climax, until she was begging for him to let her go. "Please, Sam, I want to touch you."

Soon his warm hands fumbled with the bandanas at her wrists. "Oh, thank you." She breathed. "I need to touch you. Feel you."

She reached upward when her hands were free, but he was nowhere. "Can I take off the blindfold?"

"No," his stern voice said. "Turn over."

"On my belly?"

"Yes. Turn over on your belly and then grab the headboard again."

Her body thrumming, she did as she was told. He retied her hands as she lay prone on the bed.

"Sydney, you have one beautiful ass."

"Thank you." *I think.* What else could she say? He had

one fine backside too, but not being visually aware of it at the moment, she didn't state that fact.

One finger breached her wet channel.

"Ahhh," she moaned. Perfect.

In and out he stroked her, so slowly she thought she might go mad.

"Pull your knees up under you," he said.

She obeyed, and he added another finger. This position allowed him to go deeper, stretching and probing, filling an emptiness she hadn't known existed.

She thought she might come right there.

Again.

"Oh!" Cold again, this time against her secret opening.

No one had ever touched her there. Yet no fear consumed her. She trusted Sam.

It was another ice cube, and as it melted and the tiny rivers of water trickled between her cheeks, tickling her, she sighed. She'd never known this kind of play could be so fulfilling.

If her hands were free, she could reach between her legs and stroke her clit. She'd come for sure.

But her hands weren't free. Desire to touch herself, to touch Sam, built within her until she thought for sure she'd explode.

"Sam, please! Let me go. I need to...I need..."

"No." Still stroking her with his fingers, he replaced the ice cube with his tongue.

Ah God, soft warmth. He licked her there, in that private place, and she was thrilled. Electricity sizzled through her veins. How could this feel so good? So right?

"Mmm." His voice vibrated against the sensitive skin of her crease. "You're sweet."

The feelings coursing through her were entirely new, things she'd never imagined feeling. Images swirled through her mind's eye, of Sam taking her in her ass. Would he? She didn't know. Would she let him if he wanted to?

Oh, yes. She would.

"Ah, God!" The fingers of his other hand found her swollen clit. Only a few strokes, and the sparks coursed through her again.

How many orgasms could her body take before it shut down and couldn't take any more? She had a sneaking suspicion she would find out today.

Swirling images funneled through her mind. She and Sam riding horses together across the sprawling acres of the ranch—she and Sam making love in her hotel room at the Windsor that first night five years ago—kissing and licking Sam's cock until he exploded against her tongue—a Colorado sunset with Sam, the pink-and-orange clouds forming a heart over the mountains as they held hands, kissed, vowed to love each other forever.

All from being blindfolded, sensory deprived.

"More," he said to her. "Come for me again."

"Sam, please, I—"

"Come!" he commanded.

She imploded into the bed, her body sinking downward, floating on the bottom of a lush green sea. She was a mermaid, swinging her tail and laughing at sea creatures as her body moved inward, outward, in and out of itself.

Throbbing, pulsing, convulsing, materializing and dematerializing.

"Sam, please. I have to touch you!"

He thrust his cock into her.

He started slowly, rocking back and forth into her tight channel. In. Out. In. Out.

Oh. My. God.

She wouldn't come again. She couldn't. She knew that. But still, he felt so wonderful inside her, filled her, completed her.

"You feel so good on my cock, sweetheart," he said. "So damn good."

She moved her hips back and forth as best she cold, trying to take in more of him.

"God, I could do this forever," he said. "Your body takes mine so perfectly."

Her head sank farther into the pillow, her eyes clenched shut under the blindfold. How she loved this man.

How she trusted this man.

Trust.

She needed to find a way for him to trust her.

She needed to be with him, but it would never work unless he trusted her. She'd betrayed his trust twice. Now, as he made love to her while she lay at his mercy, thrusting into her and giving her pleasure, she vowed he would trust her again.

Somehow.

CHAPTER FOURTEEN

"I didn't know you were into that kind of sex," Sydney said, resting her head on Sam's chest.

"Truthfully, neither did I." He chuckled. "But I liked it. It was a real turn-on."

"What made you want to try it today?"

"I wanted to show you that you can trust me."

She nodded, his skin warm against her cheek. "I trust you, Sam."

He didn't say it back, and she didn't expect it. She'd have to earn that.

She'd find a way. She had to. She loved this man, and she damn well was not going to live without him.

"I want to help you, Sam."

"With what?"

"Trusting me."

He sighed. "Sweetheart, I want to trust you more than anything in the world."

"What if I helped you work it out with Mom and Dad so you could see Duke?"

He sat up, pushing her off his chest. "You still don't get it, do you?"

"Get what?"

"I don't want to just see Duke. I want to raise Duke. He's my son."

Sydney's heart sank. Nothing had changed. He was still

determined to take Duke from her parents.

"They love him."

"Of course they love him. They're his grandparents. I fully expect them to be a part of his life. But your father is not his father. I am."

"Oh, Sam. Please."

"Please what? Give up my child? I can't, Sydney. I can't."

"I want you to be part of his life. And so do they."

"Part of his life isn't good enough."

"You heard what Dallas said. The court will consider what's in the child's best interests. They won't uproot him. They'll probably give you some kind of visitation, but they won't take him away from the only parents he's ever known."

"I don't care. I have to try."

"Why? Why can't we just talk to my parents?"

"Because if I don't try, I'll never forgive myself. I've always wanted kids, Sydney, and here I find out I actually have one. A beautiful little boy. I love him, Sydney. I loved him as soon as I found out about him, but last night, seeing him lying in that hospital bed, possibly dying, I knew he was mine. My heart cried out for him. I wanted only to protect him. To take away any pain he might ever feel."

What a wonderful man. He would indeed have made an amazing father. But she had to clue him in on something. "Sam, you can't take away every pain he might ever feel. No one can. Your parents couldn't do that for you, could they?"

Sam sighed. "You're right. They couldn't. They didn't."

"No parent can."

"But I should be there for him. I love that child. I don't even know him yet, but I love him."

Sydney summoned all her emotion, all her love for Sam,

and met his gaze. "Then please don't hurt him."

He looked away from her, rose, walked out of the room, and then back in. His eyes were wet, and a streak ran down each of his cheeks.

"All right, Sydney," he said. "Let's talk to your parents."

Still naked, she jumped off the bed and ran into his arms. "Thank you, Sam. You won't regret this, I promise you. You can trust me on that."

★ ★ ★

Sam drove Sydney back to the hotel so she could get over to the grounds and work Sapphire. They had a race the next day. Sam agreed to wait a day or two before talking to her parents. He wanted Duke to get over the virus he had, and he wanted to wait until the DNA test results came in. They could be in as early as this afternoon, though he figured tomorrow was a safer bet.

He worked his horse a little, thinking he might actually compete tomorrow as planned. After all, he'd already missed one competition. His heart wasn't really in it, though. He had other stuff on his mind. Besides, with the new job he was taking with Zach, he no longer needed purse money.

Then, out of the blue, it hit him—what he wanted to do this afternoon. He went to the main house to talk to Dusty.

"Is Seanie home?"

"Yes, he's outside having a riding lesson with one of the hands."

"Good. When will he be done?"

"In a half hour or so. Why?"

"I'd like to spend the afternoon with my nephew."

"That's sweet, Sam. I'm sure he'd love it."

"We could go fishing. Or I could take him up to the rodeo to watch some of the competitions."

"He'd love that. Why don't you plan on it? Are you hungry? I can make you a sandwich."

"Yeah, as a matter of fact." Sam sat down at the kitchen table.

Dusty grabbed some deli meat out of the fridge. "It's such good news about Duke. I was really scared."

Sam nodded. "I was freaked."

"I was worried that our stupid DNA was going to make his life hard."

"You know you didn't need to worry about that. We've heard it a hundred times. There's no indication anywhere that leukemia is hereditary."

"I know, but first Mom, and then me." Dusty shook her head as she spread mustard on two slices of bread. "It sure seems to be in our family."

"Luckily, you are cured. And Duke is clean. Thank God."

"I shook all last night till we got your call."

"I know, Dust. I'm sorry."

"Don't be. It's part of my life. Every time I take Seanie in for a sick visit, I'm scared to death they're going to say he has the damn thing."

"Sean is fine. He'll always be fine. And so will Duke."

"God, I hope you're right." She set the sandwich on a plate and placed it before him.

He smiled. "Of course I'm right."

"Eat your sandwich. Sean'll be done soon, and you can have your uncle's outing."

Mmm, good old McCray roast beef. And a date with his

nephew. Just what he needed. Some five-year-old boy time.

If he couldn't lavish his love on his son, he could lavish it on his adorable nephew.

★ ★ ★

Sydney ached with exhaustion. She and Sapphire had had a good workout. She'd gone back to hotel, taken a long hot shower, and decided to check in on Duke.

She walked down the hall and knocked on the door to her parents' hotel room.

No response.

Had they gone out? Hmm. Duke was surely still not himself. When Sydney had called this morning, her mother said he'd slept well and was doing better, but Sydney had assumed they'd be staying in today.

She called her mother's cell phone. No answer. Her father's. No answer. Well, if they were at the rodeo, no doubt they couldn't hear the phones over all the commotion.

This was good news. Duke was obviously feeling better. Sydney checked her watched. Nearly dinner time. No wonder her tummy was putting up a fuss.

She had a great idea. She'd call Sam and invite him for dinner. They could go to the Blue Bird on Main. Too bad she didn't have a kitchenette in her hotel room. She'd love to cook for him.

But wait, he had a kitchen in his guest house. Would it be presumptuous to invite herself over to cook him dinner? Heck, they'd shared stuff a lot more intimate that a home-cooked meal this morning in bed.

She dialed his number and her pulse raced when he

answered.

"Hi, Sam. It's me."

"Hello, Sydney."

"I was wondering...well, Duke's doing better and Mom and Dad took him out, so I was thinking... Would you like to have dinner with me?"

"I'm afraid I have company right now," he said.

"Oh." Her heart sank. "I'm sorry. I didn't mean to interrupt."

"You're not interrupting. I was about to cook a great meal of mac and cheese for my nephew. We would love to have you join us."

"Oh." *Thank God. He's not with another woman.* "I don't want to intrude."

"Who's intruding? Sean and I had a fun afternoon riding horses together. And now we're famished, aren't we, buddy?"

Childish laughter rang in the background.

"Well, then, I'd love to join you. But I was hoping I could cook you dinner."

"I'm afraid Seanie has his heart set on Uncle Sam's famous mac and cheese, but you could make dessert."

"Perfect," Sydney said. "I'll pick up groceries on the way. What would you like?"

"Let's ask the guest of honor. What would you like for dessert, bud?"

"Something chocolate!"

Sam laughed. "Did you hear that?"

"I sure did. I know just what to make. One of my specialties. I'll be there in an hour."

"Mac and cheese should be almost done by then."

They hung up and Sydney headed to the grocery and

purchased ingredients for chocolate mousse. It didn't take long to make, and it could chill while they ate.

"Oops," she said out loud. Chocolate mousse had raw eggs in it. Not the best for a five-year-old. Now what? She'd promised chocolate. She grabbed cocoa, eggs, sugar, and a pint of premium vanilla ice cream.

Flourless chocolate torte to the rescue. All she needed was a round cake pan. Hopefully the guest house had one. On second thought, she headed to the housewares section and grabbed a disposable foil pan just in case.

And off to Sam's.

She found herself humming a lively tune as she drove, looking forward to spending time with Sam and his nephew. It would be almost like—

Almost like she and Sam making dinner for Duke—had she told him and had they decided to raise him together, of course.

She'd made what she thought was the best decision at the time. No use crying over spilled milk.

She arrived to a smiling Sean on the front stoop. He had hair like his mother and light blue eyes. A beautiful little boy, just like her Duke.

"Are you Sydney? Uncle Sam said you were coming."

"Yes, I am. And you're Sean. I remember you from your mom and dad's party."

"You're pretty."

"Why thank you."

"Come on in."

"Thank you very much."

Sean led the way. "She's here, Uncle Sam, and she's pretty!"

Sam's laugher rang from the kitchen. "Yes, she certainly is."

"Mmm. It smells great in here. The savory aroma of cheddar cheese wafted to her nose.

"It's almost ready."

"Okay. I just need about ten minutes to whip up my dessert. It can bake while we eat."

"Have at it. The kitchen is pretty well-stocked. Sean and I will stay out of your way."

Sydney put together her flourless torte with ease and got it in the oven. By the time she was done, Sam was spooning out globs of piping hot mac and cheese onto plates.

He poured a glass of milk for Sean and opened a bottle of Gewürztraminer and poured two glasses. He handed one to Sydney. "I hope you like white wine."

"I like most wine," she said. "Thank you."

They sat down and dug in.

"Mmm, this is delicious," Sydney said.

"My own personal recipe. I've been on my own up at the ranch for the last five years. I had to learn to cook. This is actually made with four different cheeses."

"Let me guess. Cheddar, of course, Monterey jack, parmesan, and..."

"It's the last one that always tricks people up."

"Wait a minute, I'll get it." She took another bite. "Is it Roquefort?"

"You're as smart as you are beautiful." He grinned.

"What's rockport?" Sean asked.

"It's just a kind of cheese," Sam said. "It's good, isn't it?"

"Yum," he said, holding out his plate. "Can I have more?"

"You sure can."

"I'll get it, Sam." Sydney stood. "You want more milk too, honey?"

"Yes, please."

She rose a few moments later to take her torte from the oven. "This needs to cool for a few minutes. Then we'll have it hot with a scoop of vanilla ice cream on top. Does that sound good?" she asked Sean.

"Sounds great!"

She smiled. What a cutie! He was so much like Duke. They were cousins after all. She couldn't wait for the two of them to get to know each other.

Sean got up to run around and Sydney asked Sam, "Did you hear about the DNA test yet?"

"No. Tomorrow, probably."

"Well, you and I both know what it'll say."

"Yes, but I want to have it in hand before I talk to your parents. I agreed to do this, Sydney, but only if they're willing to be fair."

"They'll be fair," she said, hoping to God she was right. "They won't want to put Duke through a lawsuit or anything."

Sam shook his head. "I don't want to do that either. I really don't. I'm just not sure there's any other way, especially if they won't cooperate."

"They'll cooperate. The only thing is, you're going to have to meet them halfway."

"I just wish you'd told me five years ago. Then we wouldn't have this problem."

"We've been through that, Sam. I made the decision I thought was right at the time."

"You made a mistake."

"Yes, I can see now that I did. But that's all hindsight and retrospect. At the time, I had no idea you'd want to know. I thought I was doing you a favor."

"Yes, I've heard your side of it. We don't need to go there again."

She sighed. "Let's have our dessert. Go on and call Sean in, and I'll serve it up."

Sean pronounced the dessert a success, and Sydney laughed as she wiped the chocolate off his cute little face.

"It's getting about to be your bedtime, bud," Sam said.

"No, I don't wanna go."

"Why doesn't he spend the night here with you?" Sydney said.

"Now that's a good idea. Would you like that, partner?"

"Eggs and hash browns in the morning?"

"Of course."

"Then yeah! Can Sydney stay too?"

Sydney's cheeks warmed. She'd like nothing better than to spend another night with Sam, but not with his little nephew in the house. It wouldn't look right.

"Not this time, I'm afraid," she said. "I need to be getting back to my hotel. I'm competing tomorrow." She looked at Sam. "Aren't you competing tomorrow?"

"I've decided not to," he said.

"Really? Why not?"

"I'm moving here as soon as I get things settled at the ranch in Montana."

"Moving here? Why?"

"Uncle Sam's gonna live here with us," Sean said.

"Zach offered me a job as ranch foreman along with a nice ownership interest. I couldn't turn him down. Plus, I'll get to see my sis and this little guy a lot more often." He grabbed

Sean and gave him a rough noogie.

Sean laughed, squirming. "Stop that!"

"What's that have to do with not competing tomorrow?"

"I'm thirty-three years old. I've broken a few ribs over the years, strained a lot of muscles. I'm not the competitor I was ten years ago. It's time to say goodbye to that life. I've got a chance to make a great living out here, and I want to focus on that."

Sydney nodded. She couldn't imagine giving up racing. Of course she was younger at twenty-four. But Dusty had given it up at twenty-three when she got pregnant with Sean.

She didn't need to think about that. She wasn't pregnant. Hadn't been in a while. And she didn't have a family to think about other than her parents and Duke, and they relied on her purse money.

But had she made the right choice? Maybe she should have stopped racing long ago and raised her son.

She'd been young, no doubt. But she'd also been selfish, and her selfishness was coming back to bite her in the butt. She'd made things much harder on her parents and Duke than she'd ever intended. And on Sam. And even on herself.

For a moment again, she imagined Sean as Duke and herself and Sam as the happily married parents.

Could it have happened then?

She sighed. She'd never know.

She stood. "As much as I hate to say goodbye, I have to be going. Thank you so much for dinner," she said to Sam. Then, to Sean, "I had a great time hanging out with you. I hope we can do it again sometime."

"Okay, as long as you bring chocolate."

She laughed and ruffled his hair. "It's a deal."

"I'll walk you out," Sam said.

"You don't need to bother."

"It's no bother. The critter'll be fine in here for a minute, won't you?

"Yup."

He walked her to her car and took both hands in his. "I'm glad you came. Dessert was delicious. But"—he leaned in—"not half as delicious as you are."

He pressed his mouth to hers in a soft kiss.

She parted her lips and the kiss deepened, but he pulled back. "I have to get back inside."

"I know."

"I'm glad you came."

"Sam, I hope you know we will work this out somehow. My parents are not unreasonable people."

He nodded. "I've given you a hard time. I don't mean to. It's just—"

She put her fingers to his mouth, silencing him. "Don't. I understand. Good night."

"Good night."

He stood outside until she had backed out and was on her way down the winding road of the McCray Ranch, heading toward the county road.

She pulled out her cell phone and hit her mother's number on speed dial. She'd be back at the hotel soon, but she wanted to check on Duke.

"What?" she said aloud.

Her heart sped up and her throat constricted. Nausea worked its way up her esophagus. Quickly she hit "end" and redialed, this time punching in the actual numbers.

Her tummy plummeted as she listened to the same

message.

This number is no longer in service.

CHAPTER FIFTEEN

She pulled to the side of the road, frantic, and tried her father's number.

Same message.

She gunned the engine and sped back to the hotel. She rushed in and stopped at the front desk. "Roy and Carrie Buchanan and their son—did they check out?"

The clerk checked his computer. "No, ma'am. They're scheduled to be here six more days."

Thank goodness.

Must be a glitch with one of the cellular towers in the area. She took the elevator up and walked to her room. She wanted to check on Duke, so she crossed the hall to her parents' room and knocked.

No response.

She knocked louder. It was after ten o'clock. They couldn't still be out with Duke, could they? After he'd been so sick just the night before?

She knocked again, this time nearly putting her fist through the door. "Mom, Dad." She didn't want to yell. It was late, and some of the other guests were no doubt in bed.

She let out a breath. Those invisible bugs were crawling up her arms again—something didn't feel right about this. But surely her parents were taking good care of Duke. They probably ran into some friends or something at the rodeo and were up talking. Duke was no doubt snoozing on his mother's lap this very minute.

Sydney was exhausted herself, and she had a competition tomorrow. Best get to bed.

She went to her own room, undressed, washed up, and fell into bed.

She'd check on her baby in the morning.

★ ★ ★

At the first light of dawn, Sydney woke, her heart pounding.

What was going on?

She couldn't remember having a nightmare. Why was she so on edge?

Duke. She was worried about Duke. She pulled on a robe, walked across the hall, and knocked again on her parents' door. Still no answer.

This was getting freaky.

She went back to her room and tried both of their cell numbers again. She got the same troubling message. Their numbers were no longer in service.

That nauseated feeling plagued her again.

Something was very wrong.

She called to the front desk and found her parents had still not checked out.

Then she called Sam. Just to say good morning, she said in as cheery a voice as she could muster. She didn't want to alarm him. It was just a test to check the cellular service in the area, which was obviously working just fine.

Her heart sped. What the hell was going on?

She'd taken the rental car yesterday. Where were they?

Suddenly, she had a terrible thought. What if they were

in their room and couldn't get to the door? Oh no! What if something horrible had happened?

She nearly lost what little was left in her stomach as she pulled on some jeans and a shirt and raced down to the front desk.

"I need you to open my parents' room," she said.

"Ma'am?" The clerk looked at her with a concerned face.

"You've told me they haven't checked out, but I don't have a clue where they are. They didn't answer last night and they're not answering the door this morning. They're not answering the phone."

"Maybe they stayed out all night. Sometimes, adults do that."

"Not adults with a five-year-old little boy. Please do this for me. Humor me."

"Okay, okay. I'll have someone from security check it out."

A few minutes later, Sydney followed a security official to the door of her parents' room. He knocked firmly. "Mr. Buchanan? Mrs. Buchanan?"

"I told you they're not answering."

"All right, miss, simmer down. We're going in." He slid a card through the lock and opened the door.

Sydney rushed past him into the room.

Her heart dropped. No suitcases in sight. The beds had been made, obviously by housekeeping yesterday. They had not been slept in.

She ran into the bathroom. Nothing but a few half-used bottles of hotel shampoo and lotion. Everything else was gone.

What on Earth?

"Looks like they left, ma'am," the security guy said.

"But they didn't. The clerk said they didn't check out."

"Then they didn't check out but they left anyway. It happens."

"You don't understand. They're booked here for five more days. For the rodeo."

"I guess they decided to go home."

"But they would have told me." She plunked down on one of the beds. "This isn't good. This isn't good at all. Something is definitely wrong."

"I wish I could help you, but I need to get this room closed back up. I'll need to notify the front desk. They may have skipped out on their bill."

"They didn't," Sydney said, her head in her hands. "They prepaid for the rodeo. Oh my God."

"I'm sorry, ma'am. I don't know what else to say."

"It's all right. Just go."

"I need to ask you to leave this room."

"Can I just look around first? See if they might have left something behind? I need to know what's going on."

"Okay, you can have ten minutes."

She used every millisecond of those ten minutes, scouring every millimeter of the room for something—anything—to clue her in on what had happened.

Nothing.

No evidence of any struggle. No evidence of anything at all, except that they were gone.

"Thank you," she said to the security guy. She walked soberly back to her own room.

She dialed the land line to their home in Carson City. No answer, of course. If they'd driven, they wouldn't have gotten back there yet. Or maybe they would have if they'd driven all night. Or they could have caught a red-eye flight.

God, now what?

If they flew, the airport would have those records, right? But would she be able to access them?

Where were they?

Visions of a masked gunman taking them hostage tormented her. Perhaps they were bound and gagged at this very moment in the back of a truck somewhere.

Perhaps Duke... *Dear Lord, Duke!*

Who could help her?

Sam. Sam would help her.

Her skin chilled when a horrible thought crossed her mind.

What if her parents had skipped town with Duke? To keep Sam away from him?

They wouldn't.

Would they?

No, of course not. They were also keeping Sydney away from him, and they would never do that.

Yet none of this made sense. If they'd been abducted, their cell phones would still work. They might not answer, but the numbers would still go through.

More importantly, there'd be evidence of some sort of struggle. Something would have been left behind. Maybe the gunman had made them pack everything up—

No.

Her body went limp. In her heart, she knew the truth.

They had left.

Her parents were good people. They wouldn't have done this if they hadn't thought it completely necessary. Desperation had obviously fueled them.

What could she do? She could wait for them to show up

at home. They'd have to answer the land line sooner or later.

If, indeed, they went home at all.

The thought nagged her. If they'd canceled their cell numbers, they probably weren't headed home.

They were headed somewhere else. Somewhere Sam—and no one else—would ever find them.

Sydney buried her face against the palms of her hands. How had it all come to this? She swallowed. She could go after them, look for them. Not bother Sam until she knew something concrete.

No. She couldn't do that to Sam. She couldn't keep this from him. Not only would he have one more reason not to trust her, but more importantly, this was Sam's business. He had a right to know.

She'd taken away his rights five years ago. She could not do it again. She had to find Sam and tell him.

Her heart sank when a truth struck her in a black haze.

She'd tell Sam what happened—that her parents had skipped town and taken Duke with them. That they hadn't told her they were leaving and they'd canceled their cell phone numbers.

It was the truth and nothing but the truth.

There was only one problem.

He wouldn't believe her.

CHAPTER SIXTEEN

"How could they?" Sam paced around the living room of his guest house. "How could they just pack up a sick little kid and leave?"

"I don't know, Sam. I guess they thought they had no choice."

"Why don't you tell me the truth for once, Sydney," he said. "You sent them on their merry way, and now you're lying to me, aren't you?"

Just what she'd been afraid of. He didn't believe her. "I swear to you that's not true. Call the hotel if you want. I was frantic this morning looking for them. Their cell phones have been disconnected, for God's sake. I had nothing to do with this."

"You never wanted me in the picture from the beginning."

"That's not true!" Tears streamed down her cheeks. "I've explained all that."

"Why should I believe any of this?"

She sat down. What could she say? " Sam. I can only tell you it's the truth."

"If you were in my shoes, would you believe it?"

She shook her head. "I honestly don't know. And that's the cold hard truth."

He softened a little. The fire in his dark eyes turned to ash. "God." He sat down on the couch and buried his head in his hands. "This is all my fault."

Sydney went to him, tried to comfort him, but he shook her away. "Don't."

"It's not your fault, Sam. It's mine. This all began when I made a horrible mistake. I chose not to tell you about Duke, and I chose not to tell my parents who the father was. I thought I was protecting you, but I see now that I was young and naïve. I'm sorry. You had a right to know your son."

No response.

She put her arms around his shoulders, tried to hold his unresponsive body. "I love you, Sam. I have never stopped loving you."

Still no response.

"We will find them, and we will work something out."

He lifted his head. "You said they'd be willing to talk to me."

She shook her head. "I thought they would. This behavior isn't like them at all. I'm not sure why they left, but they must have thought they had good reason. I can guarantee you one thing. They would never in a million years harm Duke. We can at least know that he's safe."

"We need to call Dallas. Or the cops."

"No. Dallas and the cops can't do anything. They are Duke's legal parents. In the eyes of the law, they haven't done anything wrong."

"I can't accept that. Damnit." He stood. "I'm calling Dallas."

Sydney sat, numb, as he spoke to his brother-in-law for a few minutes. When he hung up, his eyes were glazed over.

"You're right. The cops won't touch this. We have nothing to stand on."

"I'm sorry."

"Our only option is to hire a private investigator. Chad knows a good one who he uses all the time."

"I don't think we need a PI. We can find them. Where could they go? They don't have a lot of disposable cash. Most of our money is tied up in the ranch. We're not in financial straits or anything, but we're not rolling in it either. I wanted to win a few purses here because we can really use the money."

"Aren't you supposed to compete today?"

She nodded. "I can't. Not now. My head's not in it." She hoped he understood, though she could use the money now more than ever.

Man up, Syd. Her father's voice spoke in her thoughts. He'd said those words to her older brother, Blake, many times, but never to her. They rang true for her now.

She stood. "I've changed my mind. I have enough time to get over there and get ready. I'm competing today. We need the purse money to find Duke."

He nodded. "I've got my job here, but of course I haven't gotten paid yet. Most of my money is tied up in the ranch in Montana. I'm in the same boat your parents are, but I think I know where I can get some fast cash."

"How?"

"I'll ride Zach's bull."

Sydney jerked. "You're crazy! That bull almost killed both Dusty *and* Zach five years ago. I won't allow it."

"You won't allow it? Oh, that's rich."

"You're not a bull rider. You're a bronc buster. There's a huge difference."

"It can't be that different. I'm a hell of a bronc buster. Besides, what makes you think you have any say in it?"

"Because I love you, that's why!" She threw her arms

around him and crushed her lips to his.

It was a kiss of not only passion, but fear and anxiety. They were both worried about Duke.

Electricity pulsed between them. Sam lifted her in his arms and they continued kissing, their lips and tongues sliding together in lustful rhythm.

Sydney pulled away. "I'm sorry. I know now isn't the time for this. We have to figure out what we're going to do. Plus, I have a competition this afternoon."

"There is time. I will take you to the rodeo. Now is the perfect time for this." He lifted her in his strong arms and carried her to his bedroom.

No bandanas tying her to the bed posts this time. No angry, punishing kisses. This was slow, sweet love. They kissed for a long time and then slowly undressed each other.

When Sam entered her, tears welled in her eyes. Emotion so thick she could almost see it swirled between them. She hadn't known she'd been so empty until he filled her at that moment.

She loved this man.

Suddenly, she knew she always had.

It was because of her love for him that she hadn't told him about Duke. She hadn't wanted to wreck his life, to trap him. He would not understand her logic. She wasn't sure she understood it herself. She only knew the truth of it in her heart.

His thrusts became harder, and even without the clitoral stimulation she thought necessary, an orgasm rose within her.

They came in unison, panting and heaving, until they were a mass of naked limbs tangled together, breathing heavily.

"That was amazing," Sydney said.

He grunted, his eyes closed.

"I have to get to the rodeo."

"I know. I'll take you." He didn't move.

"It's okay. I can get there myself."

"No, I want to go with you. We can talk on the way about what we're going to do."

"All right."

They showered in each other's arms and then dressed. After a quick stop at the hotel for Sydney's racing clothes, they got to the rodeo without much time to spare. Sydney had given Sapphire a workout the day before so the mare was in good shape.

She needed the purse.

She couldn't let Sam ride that huge-ass bull.

Sam left her to prepare Sapphire. He'd be in the stands, he assured her, cheering her on.

Sydney groomed Sapphire, trying like hell to concentrate on the race. Her visualization was stunted. She couldn't picture the race. She couldn't picture winning.

Instead her mind conjured images of her baby boy on the run with her parents. She'd failed Duke, and she'd failed Sam. What was she going to do?

Right now Sam seemed rational, but who knew what would happen when they finally caught up with her parents and Duke?

Damn it, Sydney, focus!

She tried to concentrate on Sapphire. Nope, wasn't working. She continued grooming on autopilot, knowing full well she should be bonding with her mare instead of ruminating. The race and the purse depended upon her and Sapphire being in perfect sync.

"That's my girl," she said to the horse. Normally she talked in soothing tones while grooming. She hadn't today. She hoped Sapphire would be okay.

Once finished, she and Sapphire headed to the arena to await the start of the race. Sydney was set to go second to last.

One by one, she watched the other racers, each time thinking they did something better than she did. She had beaten most of these racers the other day, so why was she doubting herself?

Because now there was something more at stake. Not just the purse.

Duke.

Sam.

The two most important people in her life.

She'd never have a life with both of them. Duke was her parents' son now. The most she'd ever get as the birth mother was visitation, and she could have that now as his big sister. What would Sam get?

Probably nothing.

Of course, if he married her, he could be Duke's brother-in-law. Sydney shook her head. That wouldn't be enough for Sam. And though he professed to love her, he would never marry her just to have his son. He was too honorable for that.

He had to trust her first.

She had to find a way to make him trust her.

How? How could she? She'd betrayed him in such a terrible way already. She'd kept him from his son. She wasn't sure she could ever forgive herself.

And now her parents, her beloved parents, had run rather than face losing the little boy they adored.

She had gotten herself, her son, her parents, and the man she loved into one fine mess indeed.

"Syd, you're up next," Sharla Perkins, the racer behind her, said.

Sydney jerked out of her stupor. She hadn't even seen the racers ahead of her go. She had no idea what kind of competition she was up against.

She and Sapphire headed forward.

"Next up is Sydney Buchanan of Nevada," the announcer, Mark, said. "Sydney won a handsome purse in her first race. Let's see what she can show us today."

Yeah, let's see for sure.

She closed her eyes. But instead of images of her and Sapphire, working as one, only dark visions of her parents running away appeared.

Sapphire. Must see myself with Sapphire. Why isn't this working?

No more time to stall. She had to go.

She opened her eyes, signaled to the judge, and raced forward. With the force of a tornado, Sydney took Sapphire around the first barrel perfectly. She looked straight ahead and galloped toward the second, taking Sapphire around in the opposite direction. Thank God! One more to go. She aimed toward the final barrel.

Thundering applause rushed from the stands. She could do it. She was doing it. Sam was out there watching. She'd do it for him, for Duke, for all the mistakes she'd made.

God, the mistakes...

A millisecond later, Sapphire knocked down the final barrel.

Her throat constricted, Sydney raced back and crossed the electric eye. She didn't see her time.

It didn't matter anyway. Even if she'd made her personal

best, the barrel would cost her a five second penalty. She wouldn't place.

She dismounted and petted the mare's nose. "Great job, sweetie."

A local girl approached her. "Tough break," she said.

Sydney tried to feign nonchalance. "It happens."

The girl smiled and went on her way. Sydney took Sapphire back to the stalls and cleaned her up.

After she'd taken care of the mare and blown the congestion out of her nose, hoping she'd shed her last tear, she went out into the stands to find Sam.

She walked for a while, her brain in a haze, seeing only blurred faces in front of her. No blurry Sam. When she'd nearly given up, he appeared.

"Lord," she groaned under her breath.

Next to him, jabbering in his ear, was none other than Rod Kyle.

CHAPTER SEVENTEEN

"Look," Sam said, "I'm not interested in all the documentation you have. I know the kid is mine. The DNA results will be in today, tomorrow at the latest. In fact, they might be in right now. I haven't checked my phone in a while."

"What I'm trying to tell you is that Roy and Carrie Buchanan are not who they seem to be," Rod said. "I thought for sure you'd be interested."

"You think I'd trust anything you told me?"

"Look, I get that Sydney's not going to marry me. I'm not thrilled about the gossip and shit it's going to create. My father had his own reasons for wanting me to marry her, and her family had a lot to do with it. He's livid about the broken engagement."

"What the hell would her family have to do with it? And why the fuck does your father care who you marry? Jesus Christ."

"That's what I'm trying to tell you. I found some information—"

"What exactly have you found, then? And why were you looking?"

"Fair question. I started looking to find a way to keep Sydney from breaking our engagement. My father wanted the marriage more than I did, and my father doesn't ever do anything without a reason, so I dug deeper."

"Say I want this information," Sam said. "What's it going

to cost me?"

"You need to leave Sydney. Give her up."

Sam shook his head. "You're dreaming. I have a child with that woman."

"But you're not in love with her."

"That's none of your goddamn business."

Rod's meticulously groomed eyebrows shot up. "Shit, are you telling me you've fallen for that manipulative little tramp?"

Sam grabbed Rod's collar. "You want another punch in the face? 'Cause I can sure arrange it."

"Ease up, ease up."

Sam let him go.

Rod rubbed his neck. "Christ. What a mess you've gotten yourself into."

"Nothing like the mess you're gonna be in if you ever say anything like that about Sydney again."

"Fine, fine." Rod rubbed his jaw. "Are you willing to give her up?"

"It depends on the information. Why don't you give me a preview, and I'll think about it?"

"Fair enough." Rod moved closer to him. "Sydney has an older brother."

"Yeah. Blake. He worked for one of my brothers-in-law for a while. But I already know that. Anything else?"

"Blake had a falling out with his parents some time ago. He left their ranch to make it on his own. He lived here for a while, working for your brother-in-law, and then got caught up in a scandal involving the mayor's daughter."

"Yeah, yeah, I know all that. The mayor went to prison for shooting Blake. The daughter miscarried. Tell me something I don't know."

"From here, Blake went to San Antonio and got into some real trouble with crime bosses in high places."

"So?"

"So I'd bet you don't know what caused the falling out in the first place. Why Blake left his parents."

"Probably because he's an asshole and they kicked him out. The guy's clearly a loser."

"That may be, but it has nothing to do with why he left. Blake wasn't kicked out. He left of his own accord."

"Why?"

Rod's lips curved into a sickening smile. "That's the information I have. Roy and Carrie Buchanan are not what they seem."

"Yes, you already said that."

"So will you leave Sydney?"

For that? For "Roy and Carrie aren't who they seem to be?" Not only no, but hell no.

"No, I will not leave Sydney. Now get the hell out of my sight."

"Speak of the devil," Rod said.

Sydney approached. The sadness in her dark eyes nearly broke Sam's heart.

"Nice race," Rod said.

"Fuck you," Sydney said.

"Get out of here," Sam said to Rod. "I have no more use for you."

"You have no idea what you're dealing with," Rod said.

"Then I'll figure it out on my own. Now go, before I kick your ass into next year."

Rod shrugged. "Don't say I didn't try."

"What's going on?" Sydney asked when Rod had left.

"He's a pain in the ass, but he did say something worthwhile."

"What's that?"

"I'm not sure yet. We need to talk to someone."

"Who?"

"Your brother."

"I haven't talked to Blake in years."

"He's here in town, isn't he?"

"I have no idea. Last I heard he was in San Antonio."

"No, he came back here. Harper and Amber know him."

"They're busy with wedding plans."

"True. But we can easily find him. He used to work for Chad. I'll give him a call."

"Okay. Whatever you think is best," Sydney said. "I'm going to call the foreman at our ranch and see if Mama and Daddy have come home yet. They're still not answering the land line. I'm going to call our neighbors, too."

"You do that. But first—" He pulled her to him for a hug. "I'm sorry about the race."

"No, *I'm* sorry. We needed that money, Sam."

"We'll make do. I have credit cards and a good job with Zach. We'll be fine."

"I have my purse money from the race the other day. It's in the safe in my room."

"Good. We won't use it unless we have to."

"I want to use it. This is all my fault. I want to help."

"That's sweet of you. All right. Let's make our phone calls, and then we'll go grab a bite to eat and figure out what to do next."

★ ★ ★

Blake hadn't changed a bit.

He was still a good-looking and feisty cowboy, though he seemed a bit more humble. Clearly he'd been taken down a few notches over the last several years. Happiness swelled in Sydney's heart. She hadn't realized how much she'd missed him.

Sam had gotten his number from Chad, and Blake had agreed to meet them for dinner in the privacy of Sydney's hotel room. They ordered pizza, and Blake came with a six pack of Bud.

"It's good to see you, Sis," he said. "How are Mom and Dad?"

Sydney let out a sigh. "They're fine, as far as I know."

"What's that supposed to mean?"

"We'll get to that," Sam said. "Right now we have a lot of questions for you."

"Starting with why you left home," Sydney said.

Blake took a long drink of beer. "That's a story for sure. Why, though, do you want to know now? It's been a while since I've been gone. You were expecting, I believe, when I took off."

"Yes."

"What happened to the baby?"

"It's a long story. But first you need to know that the baby is Sam's."

"What? You fucked my baby sister and left her pregnant?" Blake stood.

"Stop, stop," Sydney said. "I was a willing participant, and he didn't even know I was pregnant."

"I heard Mom and Pop adopted a kid after I left. Was

that...?"

"Yeah."

"I see. Well, spit out your story then, Sis. If you expect me to be honest with you, I expect to know why you're asking."

"Fair enough," she said.

After she and Sam had told the story, Blake opened another beer.

"Any more pizza?" he asked.

"We can order more."

"Nah, I'm fine. That's a heck of a story. Mom and Pop flew the coop, huh?"

"That's what we're assuming. Evidently they thought Sam would try to take Duke away from them."

"Yes, I can see where you might think that."

"What other reason would they have for leaving?"

"Probably none. Unless they thought you were about to uncover some stuff."

"Uncover what? What on Earth are you talking about?"

"Okay. I'm going to tell you why I left. Why our parents and I are no longer on speaking terms. And just so you know, I've missed you, Sis."

"I've missed you too."

"This is all great, but could you start talking please?" Sam said.

"Mom and Dad aren't who they appear to be," Blake said.

"That's just what Rod said." Sam opened a second beer. "What are you talking about?"

"Who's Rod?"

"My ex-fiancé," Sydney replied. "Evidently he did some digging on me and inadvertently found out something about Mom and Dad. He tried to get Sam to pay for the information, but he wouldn't. Rod's the one who told us that you weren't kicked out—that you left of your own accord."

"Rod's right."

"What could be so bad that you left your pregnant little sister behind?" Sam said.

"I felt bad about that," Blake said, "and I still do. But as long as you didn't know what I knew, I figured you were okay. But I can't tell you how much I've regretted leaving you there."

"Know what?" Sydney's heart lurched. "What in the world are you talking about, Blake?"

"Mom and Dad have kind of a Romeo and Juliet story," Blake said. "They were the children of feuding houses."

"What?"

"Didn't you ever think it was weird that we never knew our grandparents?"

"I guess I never thought about it."

"Both of our grandfathers are criminals, Sydney."

Sydney sat, numb, her mouth in an oval.

"Big bad criminals. Mafia."

No, couldn't be. "The Buchanans and the Ciancios? They're mob families?"

"You are as naïve as I was. I'd never heard of either family, but then we grew up in rural Nevada. We were ranch folk. We went to county schools. But yes, the Buchanans and the Ciancios are both mob families out of Chicago."

The pizza in Syd's stomach threatened to come up. "But our ranch—it's been in the family for generations."

"Nope. Dad bought the ranch."

Sydney's body felt limp. "He lied?"

"Syd, he's been lying to you for years."

"I can't believe it."

"Irish and Italian mob don't mix. But Mom and Dad fell in love. They weren't much older than the real Romeo and Juliet. Plus, Dad especially hated the mafia life. This gave him a great excuse to leave it behind."

"I wonder why their parents never came after them," Sydney said.

"Why would they? They weren't causing any trouble. They just wanted to be left alone."

"I guess that makes sense." Sydney took a drink of water. Sense? Really? None of this made any sense.

"So this trouble you got into in San Antonio?" Sam said.

"With a distant cousin on my mother's side, Paul Donetto. I figured I'd be safe, being family and all. I found out family doesn't mean jack to these people. When Michael killed Fredo in *The Godfather*, that was pretty close to reality."

Icy worry gripped Sydney's neck. "Are you still in trouble?"

"No. Donetto and I are even. I'm in no danger. I can't talk about it to you. There are things I'm not at liberty to divulge because I made promises to people. To friends."

Sam snorted. "You have friends now?"

"Yes, I do have friends, believe it or not." Blake turned to Sydney. "I'm telling you that Mom and Dad didn't kick me out. I left."

"Okay. Now tell us why," Sam said. "Just because Roy and Carrie came from criminals doesn't mean they *are* criminals. Why is this important?"

"In a perfect world, it wouldn't be. They'd have gone off together and made their own lives and left it all behind."

"Isn't that what they did?"

"They tried."

"And?" Sydney gulped.

"They couldn't cut it. The ranch was never very profitable. The best thing they did was get you and me trained in rodeo arts. We actually have some talent, though God knows where it came from. A long line of mobsters who could make a living in the rodeo, I guess, though they'll never know it."

"You're digressing," Sam said.

"Sorry." Blake opened another beer. "I never had any reason to suspect anything, and I didn't, but one day I was tooling around in Dad's office, looking for a paper clip. I pulled the flat drawer of his desk out a little too hard, I guess, and it ended up on the floor. As I was putting it away, the bottom gave way. Or should I say, the false bottom."

Sydney's ear perked up. "What?"

"A false bottom. Underneath the drawer was a small compartment about half an inch thick. And in it were some papers." He shook his head. "I shouldn't have looked, but I did. Curiosity go the best of me."

"What were they?"

"Bank accounts. In the Cayman Islands."

"So what?"

"The Cayman Islands are a place where people keep money that isn't necessarily obtained legally, Sydney," Sam said. "They have very strict bank secrecy laws and very strict penalties for unauthorized disclosure."

"Can't anyone bank there anyway? Like in Switzerland?"

"Of course, Sis, but an offshore account in the Caymans is a major red flag for someone like Dad, who basically, as far as I knew, was a rancher making a modest living."

"So you found the account. So what?"

"I found the account. What was also interesting was the

amount of money in the account."

"How much? Ten or twenty thousand?"

"Try nine hundred thousand," Blake said. "Here was an account in our father's name with nearly a million dollars in it, and all this time we'd been living so frugally. Not that I minded, but sheesh, you and I would compete and turn over our purses to them. Was that fair?"

Sydney shook her head. "Doesn't seem to be. Do you know where the money came from?"

"I confronted Pop about the whole thing. He told me it was none of my goddamned business and to get the hell out if I didn't like it."

"So you left."

"Not yet. I went to Mom."

"What did she say?"

"She told me about how they'd met and fallen in love when they were still kids. How they'd run away and gotten married and had me soon thereafter. They'd wanted no part of their families' criminal activities."

"So where did the money come from?"

"It's Pop's money, from a trust fund from his mother."

"And they wouldn't use it?"

"No. He told Mom it was dirty money and he wanted no part of it."

"Then why didn't they just give it to charity or something?"

"I asked that same question. She said Pop refused to. He said they never knew when they might need it."

"Oh God." Sydney's heart fell to her tummy. "They took Duke away. They might have even left the country with all that money."

"Yes, they might have. But there was still one thing that

didn't jibe. The account papers showed multiple withdrawals from the account. So if Dad refused to use the money, who made the withdrawals?"

"Did you ask Mom?"

"I did. She said I must have misread the statements. There hadn't been any withdrawals. Then she refused to discuss the matter further." Blake shook his head. "You can think what you want about me. I'm no Einstein, but for God's sake, I can read an account statement. Money had been withdrawn."

"Are you sure it was trust fund money? Mom and Dad weren't doing anything illegal, were they?"

"I wish I knew, Sis, but I don't."

Dear God.

"I didn't have the money myself to go looking into that kind of stuff. I got myself into some trouble, as you know, and every last cent I made went to bail myself out of that. All I knew is that I wanted no part of them. They let that money sit there when we had some lean years as kids, Syd. Do you remember?"

She remembered all too well. "I'm sure they had their reasons."

"Yes, they had their reasons," Blake said, "and obviously they thought those reasons made logical sense at the time. But it burns my ass that they had this money. I wanted to go to college. So did you. Remember? We could have gone to any school we wanted. They had the money. But we didn't get to go, and someone, either Mom or Dad, had been withdrawing money from that account during those years."

"We can still go to college, Blake."

"Sure we can, if we have the money. I don't have the money right now, do you?"

Sydney rose and got another bottle of water from the mini

fridge. "All I have is the twenty grand in my safe from my purse the other day. I've given everything else to Mom and Dad."

"Why, Sydney?" Blake asked. "You're of age now. You don't have to give them your money."

"I do it for Duke," Sydney said. "They adopted him and took responsibility for him. I wanted to do my part."

"We have to find them and find Duke," Sam said.

Blake rubbed his temples. "They could be anywhere, anywhere at all, if they dipped into that money."

"But the money's in the Caymans." Sydney took a sip of water. "How could they get it?"

"Online transfers, wirings, any old way. It's easy as pie to transfer money these days."

"But they didn't bring a computer, and a transfer could be traced." Sam stood and paced. "There's no way they could have— Oh my God."

"What, Sam? What?" Sydney's pulse raced.

"When was the last time you looked in your safe, Sydney?"

"Not since I put the money there. You don't think—"

But she knew exactly what Sam was thinking, and by the look on Blake's face, he was thinking the same thing.

She gulped as she keyed in the code to her safe.

Before she opened the door, she knew.

Her money was gone.

CHAPTER EIGHTEEN

This is all my fault. This is all my fault.

Sydney couldn't breathe.

A noose was squeezing her neck. Her throat constricted. Sharp fingers of acid climbed up her esophagus, threatening to choke her.

"God, what should we do?"

Blake's voice. That was Blake's voice.

"She'll be okay."

Sam's voice. *Ah, the soothing timbre of Sam's voice.* Her man. Her love.

Warm hands caressed her, dulcet tones soothed her. "It will be okay, sweetheart. We'll figure this out. We'll find our son."

Sam lifted her away from the empty safe and laid her on the bed. "Get her some more water," he said to Blake.

No water. Just Sam. Only need Sam.

And Duke. Want to see Duke.

Until now, Sydney had been sure of one thing—her parents would never hurt Duke. She'd seen the fear in her mother's eyes when they thought Duke might have leukemia. It had mirrored her own.

And her father, what had he been thinking? He had started to come around where Sam was concerned. He seemed ready to work something out.

Yet they'd left.

Only one explanation made sense. Her mother had wanted to leave. Roy Buchanan loved his wife and gave her whatever she wanted if it was within his power to do so.

Carrie was the one who was scared of Sam, not Roy.

She must have talked him into leaving.

Only one other thing could have made them leave. If they thought harm could come to Duke by staying.

But in leaving, they'd taken Duke away from Sydney as well.

From Sassy.

Tears erupted in her eyes. She wanted her baby boy. Why, oh why had she given him up?

She'd taken the easy way out. She'd given him up without really giving him up. Duke got parents who loved him and a "big sister" who doted on him.

Sam was the real loser here. He hadn't had a choice in the matter.

She had to fix this. For Duke and for Sam.

They will not harm Duke, they will not harm Duke. She repeated the mantra in her mind.

"What should we do now?" Blake said to Sam.

"I don't know. We have to find Duke. I'm scared for him now. You don't think your parents would—"

"No." Blake shook his head. "They never harmed Syd or me. They were good parents. They just never told us the truth."

The apple didn't fall far from the tree. She hadn't told Sam the truth. She felt like shit.

"Sydney?" Sam caressed her shoulder. "Are you feeling better?"

Better? That was a laugh. It would be a long time before she felt anything close to better. But she nodded anyway. They had to get on with it. "I can't believe they stole my money."

"They've been stealing our money for years, Sis," Blake said, "when they had near a million dollars in the bank."

"But they were good parents. They loved us."

He nodded. "They did, I think."

"It killed them when you left."

"I'm sure it did," Blake said, "but I hope you'll excuse me if I don't feel a whole lot of remorse about that."

Sydney nodded. She'd have a hard time forgiving her parents for what they'd done. She didn't want to hold a grudge against Blake. She had her brother back, and she wanted to keep him.

"If I'd known, Syd..."

"Known what?"

Blake cleared his throat. "If I'd known you were going to let them adopt your child, I would have come back. I would have told you." He sat down on the other side of the bed, next to her. "I'm sorry."

"I'm sorry too, Blake. You were a good brother. I should have known you had a good reason for leaving."

"It wasn't good enough. It wasn't good enough to leave my pregnant sister there."

"It's okay. We've both made mistakes. Now it's time to correct them. Will you help Sam and me find Mom and Dad?"

"Sydney," Sam said, "I'm not sure he should be involved."

"Why not?" Blake asked. "They're my parents, and the little tyke is my nephew. I wasn't there for Sydney when I should have been. I want to be there for her now."

Sam nodded. "All right. If you can help in any way, we'd appreciate it."

"I'm afraid I don't have much money to offer."

"So we're all broke," Sydney said. "Where does that leave us?"

"It leaves us my credit cards," Sam said. "I've got a little bit in the bank."

"I've got a little in the bank too," Blake said, "but I'm afraid it's damn little."

"You're both wonderful," Sydney said. "I have nothing. They stole my purse money."

"It's okay," Blake said. "You didn't know they'd do that."

"I still can't believe it."

"I can. And you will someday, trust me."

Sam shook his head. "I can't believe I was such a bad judge of character. I really thought they were good people."

"So did I," Blake said, "and in a way, they are. They just grew up around criminals. I think they're good in their hearts, but look at the examples they had."

"At least they set good examples for us," Sydney said.

"I won't argue with that, for the most part," Blake said. "But once we were old enough to handle it, they should have told us the truth about their backgrounds."

Sam nodded. "I agree. If you had known, Sydney, you would never have let them adopt Duke."

"Probably not," Sydney said. "But Duke has had a good life up until now. He's a happy little boy."

"A happy little boy who is now God knows where," Blake said. "For all we know, they've cut his hair off or dyed it so no one will recognize him."

"No! Not his beautiful hair." Sydney burst into tears. "His hair is just like yours, Sam."

Sam caressed her forearm. "It'll grow back. We'll find him."

Yes. They'd find him. They had to.

But there would be a cost.

The mother and father she'd loved and adored for twenty-four years were now strangers to her.

★ ★ ★

"Let her sleep," Sam said to Blake. "We can figure this out in the morning."

"I still can't get over them taking her money right out of her safe. How did they figure out the combination?"

Sam shook his head. "Got me. Maybe they know the numbers she uses. Hell if I know."

"They could have gotten security to open it."

"Nah. Sydney talked to security in depth when she couldn't find her parents. They would have told her. Plus, Sydney's an adult. Security can't open a safe for anyone else, not even her parents."

"Yeah, you're probably right."

"Do you have any idea where they might go first?" Sam asked.

"Nope. Maybe to the Caymans to get the money. They were smart not to try here. They know that I know about the account and that we'd try to trace it."

"So I suppose the fact that you know is going to make them harder to track."

"I'm afraid so. Sorry about that."

"Don't be. If not for you, we'd have no idea where to start. Sydney called the folks on the neighboring ranch. They said as far as they knew, your parents hadn't returned. They were going to go over and check. I don't think they've called her back yet." Sam scratched his head, thinking. "There's something that just doesn't quite seem right to me about this situation."

"What?"

"I can't believe your parents considered me that big of a threat. I mean, they're the legal parents, and Dallas McCray told me that courts will consider the best interest of the child first, before my interests or anyone else's. Duke has been living with them his whole life, and to uproot him would not be in his best interests. I love my son, and I want him, but even I can see how the court would see this."

"Yeah. So?"

"So why would they run? They don't seem the type."

"But they are the type, Sam. They ran from their families when they were young so they could be together."

"Yes, but their families are criminals. I'm not a criminal."

"But you pose a threat, just like their families did. It really makes perfect sense if you skew your reasoning just a little."

"You mean think like people who were raised by criminals."

"Exactly."

"I suppose so." Sam paced the floor. "And when you explain it that way, it does make sense. Still, it just doesn't feel right."

"Okay. Say I'm wrong. Say they didn't run. Then what could have happened?"

Sam plunked on a chair. "That's just it. I'm not sure."

"Is there anyone else who might have an interest in Duke? In my parents?"

"Only your grandparents, but they've left them alone all this time." Sam let out a huff of air. *Think, Sam. Think.*

And a light bulb lit over his head.

"There is one other person."

CHAPTER NINETEEN

No, no, no! You can't have my son!

Sydney struggled against the arms holding her, jerking her.

She opened her eyes. Sam sat next to her, gently tugging on her.

Thank God. It had only been a nightmare.

"I'm sorry to wake you, sweetheart, but Blake and I need to talk to you."

She rubbed the sleep out of her eyes. "Okay. What about?"

"Rod Kyle."

"Rod? Why? He's old news."

"We're not so sure, Sis," Blake said. "Sam and I have been talking, and it's not completely out of the realm of reality that he might be involved in this."

"He has no interest in Duke."

"No, but he has an interest in you."

"He'll get over me. He doesn't love me. He never did."

"No, but he's used to getting what he wants, and for whatever reason, right now he wants you."

"He's not going to get me."

"I know that, but it's not only him. It's his dad. His dad wanted the marriage. You saw him talking to me after your race, remember?"

"Yeah."

"He knows about your parents. He told me they weren't

who they seemed to be. He offered me information on the condition I stay away from you."

"Goddamn him!"

"Hold the phone. I told him to fuck off. But it's clear now that he knows about your parents and their links to the criminal families. Do you think it's possible he could have something to do with their disappearance?"

Sydney shook her head. "I doubt it."

"Are you sure?"

"What would he have to gain by forcing them away? Me? I don't think so. He knows about Duke, and he knows how much I love him."

"Yes, but think about it. He could be trying to make things worse for us. He already knows you've lied to me twice."

"I don't know. Maybe." Sydney rubbed her temples. Her brain was mush right about now. She didn't want to think about Rod Kyle. Or her parents, for that matter. Their relationship would never be the same. She just wanted Duke.

How could she have made such a mistake? She'd given her little boy—her most precious thing on the planet—to her parents. She'd trusted them with him.

And now this.

"I think we need to contact Kyle," Blake said. "Sam may be onto something."

"Whatever you two think is best." Sydney yawned. Her body needed sleep. Her brain needed sleep. But when she did sleep, it was fitful, fragmented with nightmares and horrific visions.

"I need to get back to the ranch," Sam said.

"I should be going too," Blake agreed. "It's late, and we have a lot to do in the morning."

"You guys aren't really thinking about leaving me alone? Please don't." Fear, though she knew it irrational, coursed through Sydney's veins.

"I need Kyle's phone number," Blake said.

"Look in my cell." Sydney tossed it to him.

Blake fiddled with the phone and entered a number into his own. He tossed it to Sam. "You want it?"

Sam nodded. "I'm going to call him tonight, on the way home."

Christ, he really is leaving me. "Please, Sam. Stay with me."

"That's my exit cue," Blake said. "I don't need to watch my little sister get it on."

Sam let out laugh that sounded forced. "Nothing's happening." He tossed his cell phone to Blake. "Put your number in mine. I'll contact you in the morning."

Blake put in the number and then tossed the phone back. "Sounds good. Take care of her, will you?"

"I will."

Good, maybe that meant he was staying.

Blake shut the door behind him.

"I'm going to go out in the hall for a few minutes and call Rod," Sam said.

"Stay here. You can put him on speaker." No, she didn't want to talk to Rod. She'd rather be hung by her toenails on a clothesline, but she had to know if he knew anything.

"Let me handle this," Sam said. "You relax. I promise I'll tell you everything."

She relented. Relaxing was out of the question, of course, but not dealing with Rod sounded like heaven on Earth at the moment.

Sam left the room.

Sydney lay on the bed. She wanted to cry. She wanted to cry for her parents whom she didn't know at all, it turned out. She wanted to cry for her big brother, who'd had a reason for leaving after all. She wanted to cry for Sam, from whom she'd kept such a terrible secret for so many years. How would he be able to trust her? And mostly she wanted to cry for her beautiful little boy whom she might never see again. Might never hear his bubbly laughter, might never hear his sweet little voice call her "Sassy."

Was she truly all cried out? Had she become numb?

Sam entered about ten minutes later. "He says he has no clue where they are. But get this, he's offered to help us locate them."

"Don't trust him," Sydney said.

"Don't worry. You want to know his price for his help?"

"What?"

"You."

Sydney's tummy tumbled. What was it with this guy? Couldn't he take no for an answer?

But she sighed. "Take his help if you need it, Sam. I will go back with him if it means Duke comes home safely."

"No, you will not. Besides, I don't believe for a minute that he knows anything. He let something slip that made me figure out why he and his father are so anxious for this marriage. Evidently his father got involved in some bad business deals with bad people. Mob, Syd. That's why Rod's father wants this marriage. He figures with you in the family, he can keep them off his back."

"Still, if he can help us find Duke—"

Sam shook his head. "I won't put you in that position. You

are not a piece of property he can own. You are no one's price."

Warmth coursed through her. He was right, of course. But to hear the words and see the fierce look of possession on his face made her think he might be able to forgive her. Perhaps their love had a chance.

She yawned. "I'm so sleepy."

"I know, baby. I'm gonna get out of here and let you rest."

Her body quivered. Being alone scared the hell out of her. "Please don't. I mean, please stay with me."

"Syd..."

"I won't come on to you. I promise. You can sleep in the other bed if you want. I just can't be alone."

He nodded. "I don't relish being alone tonight ether, truth be told." He stalked toward her. "And I don't relish sleeping in the other bed."

★ ★ ★

Sydney woke in Sam's arms. They hadn't made love, just held each other, and it had been perfect.

Or it would have been, if not for everything else going on.

Her cell phone vibrated on the nightstand and she picked it up. Her neighbors from the adjacent ranch.

"Sydney," Marcia Tucker said, "Jay went over early this morning. No one's home. The foreman hasn't heard from your parents. He hadn't checked his cell yet, so that's why he hasn't called you back."

"Thanks, Marsh. I'm sorry I bothered you."

"Not a problem. Is everything okay?"

"I'm not sure yet. I'll keep you posted."

Sydney ended the call as Sam began to stir next to her.

"That was my neighbor," she told him. "Mom and Dad aren't home, and the foreman hasn't seen them or heard from them."

"I'm not surprised." He held his arms open and she snuggled into them. "We'll find them, sweetheart. I promise."

"Where do we start? It'll be like looking for a needle in a haystack."

"I know. We need to look for clues. They must have left something behind."

"The only clue we have is the bank account in the Caymans," Sydney said.

"That'll be our starting point. Of course they can have the money wired anywhere. We need a good hacker."

"And a PI."

"Chad knows a great one. I'll give him a call and get his number. He knows his way around computers too. He got into Dusty's medical records a while back."

"What? That's illegal."

"That's my point. The guy can do pretty much anything. He's probably a good place to start. In the meantime"—he ogled her—"I need a shower. How about you?"

"I could use one," she said, "but I'm not in the mood to... you know."

"I understand. You want to go first?"

"You go ahead. I want to lie here for a few minutes."

Sam gave her a quick kiss on the cheek and traipsed to the shower.

Sydney closed her eyes as the whoosh of the water met her ears. Sam in the shower. Naked. Warm water pulsating on his amazing body, soothing his fatigued muscles. He was so beautiful. So masculine.

So perfect in every way.

She so didn't deserve him.

Her eyes misted. She was tired of crying. If only she had told Sam the truth when she was pregnant, none of this would have happened. Maybe he would have wanted her and the baby. Maybe they would have fallen in love then.

Maybe, maybe, maybe...

She needed him. Needed his body close to hers, needed the comfort of his loving touch.

She got up and went into the bathroom. "It's me," she said.

"You okay, baby?"

"Yeah, I just—" She sighed. "You want some company?"

He pulled the shower curtain back. His sandy hair was wet and matted down, his golden body covered in gleaming water. She wanted more than company. She wanted him inside her.

"If you come in here all naked and wet, I may not be able to keep my hands to myself."

"I'm sorta counting on that."

She pulled off her robe and entered. Mmm, the warm water soothed her tired body. Sam pulled her close to him for a kiss.

It was a sweet kiss, a comforting kiss, just what Sydney needed.

As they kissed, he lifted her and eased her open with his hard cock.

She was tight, and her channel offered resistance at first. Sam didn't force it. Just held her in his strong arms and eased her down gently until she took all of him.

How good it felt. How right.

He lifted her up and down, oh so gently and so slowly, his groans music to her ears.

"Yes, Sam, yes. That's so nice. So good."

He moaned in response.

His strength was more of a comfort than a turn-on at the moment. His presence a salve, a healing ointment.

She didn't plan to climax, didn't even want to, so when the explosion sneaked up on her, it was a welcome surprise.

He continued his slow movements as she spasmed against him, and when she finished, he pulled her down hard on his erect cock.

"Yeah, baby. God, you feel good."

When he went limp and slacked against the wall of the shower stall, she slid down his body until her feet hit the wet floor. She leaned against him, fearing her legs would wobble. After a few minutes, she had her footing and she pushed backward to look into his warm brown eyes.

"Thank you," she said.

He smiled, his own eyes glazed over. "It was wonderful. You are wonderful."

"We are wonderful. Together."

Disappointment crept into her when he didn't respond, but she refused to let it spoil the beauty of what had just occurred between them.

They were right together. He would see that eventually.

I will hold onto that belief. She had to. She wasn't sure she could go on if she didn't.

Sam was done washing so he left the stall, leaving Sydney to finish her shower alone.

When she finished, toweled off, and went into to bedroom, Sam was already dressed.

"Your cell rang," he said.

"It was probably Blake. Why didn't you answer it?"

"Not my place." He tossed it to her.

"Hmm, not Blake after all. In fact, not a number or an area code I recognize. Looks like whoever it was left a voicemail." She quickly dialed voicemail.

Sydney, it's Dad. Your mother's in the hospital in Branson. I'm catching a flight and bringing Duke home to you.

CHAPTER TWENTY

"I'm sorry, Sam," Doug Cartwright, the county sheriff, said. "I can't arrest the man when he gets off the plane. He took his own son away. That's not a crime."

Sam took a sip of his coffee. He and Sydney sat with Doug at Rena's Coffee Shop. Sam had called Doug after Sydney had told him about Roy's voicemail.

Now what? Sam drummed his fingers on the table until a jolt went through him. "Hey, stealing's a crime around here."

"Sure is," Doug said.

"He took Sydney's purse money from her barrel race."

"That's a horse of a different color," Doug said. "Tell me more."

Sydney's hand touched his arm. "No, Sam."

"No, what?"

"I'm sorry. I can't have my father arrested and thrown in jail. I won't press charges for the money."

Is she serious? Smoke threatened to come right out his ears. "Are you kidding, Syd? That's all we've got."

Tears welled in Sydney's eyes. "He's my father. And he's bringing Duke back."

"Jesus H. Christ."

"He'll have an explanation, I'm sure of it. My mother's in the hospital. I don't even know what's wrong with her. I'm worried."

"Worried? After what they did?"

"They're still my parents."

"Sydney, they've been lying to you your whole life."

"I know, I know." She sniffed. "And I'm sure they thought they had a good reason."

"Fuck their good reasons. Did they have a good reason for taking your son away? For stealing your money?"

"I'm sure they thought they did."

Doug's police radio buzzed. "Excuse me," he said and headed to another table.

Sam said nothing, just stared at the beautiful woman who'd stolen his heart—and his son. How could he reconcile any of this? And now she was turning a blind eye to her father's theft. How could she? After all her parents had done? All the lies? How could she get past all that?

How could anyone get past that?

Sam shook his head slowly. How could he get past Sydney's lies?

As if reading his mind, she said, "I never actually lied to you, Sam."

Well, she had him there. She didn't lie. She just didn't tell him, first about the child five years ago, and then about her engagement to Rod Kyle.

Nope, she wasn't getting away with that one. "Omission is betrayal. Case closed." He stood.

Doug walked back toward the table. "I have to get going. Are we done here?"

Sam looked down at Sydney. "You're not pressing charges?"

Sydney shook her head.

"Then, yes, we're done here." Sam walked out the door, his own words ringing in his ears. They had so many meanings.

He wanted to look back, see Sydney's face. Would she come after him? He didn't know. His car wasn't far. His walk turned into a jog and then a sprint. He got into his car and shut the door.

He didn't look to see if Sydney was behind him. Nope, he looked only ahead.

Ahead to Denver. He'd go to the airport, wait for all the flights from Branson, and he'd have it out with Roy Buchanan once and for all.

Driving to Denver was usually relaxing, full of natural scenic beauty. He hardly ever saw another vehicle on the country roads. Normally Sam loved driving through the canyons, loved the fresh aroma of pine. Today he appreciated none of that. His nerves were on edge. He wasn't sure what he'd do to Roy when he saw him. His fists itched to pummel the bastard, but he'd have the boy with him. Sam had to think about Duke.

Duke.

His son.

His and Sydney's son.

If only things had been different. If Sydney had told him. Perhaps they could have started their life together five years ago, and today Duke would be their son. Maybe they'd have had another.

Who knows?

He'd never know.

He loved Sydney. She touched a part of him that no other woman had. Making love to her was like a beautiful symphony. It was perfection.

But they could never be together.

Love without trust was nothing.

Nothing at all.

The semitruck came out of nowhere. To avoid collision, Sam, at eighty miles per hour, drove off the two lane road into the ditch. His windshield shattered, and a loose board from the fence he hit broke through it, scattering shards of glass all over him. Barbed wire from the cattle fence poked through and gouged his face and eyes.

Searing pain shot through him.

Move. I've got to move.

Then nothing.

★ ★ ★

"Sam! Oh my God, Sam!"

The country road was dead. Sydney had been driving to Denver to find Sam. Where else would he have gone? To the airport to find Roy and Duke.

Fear had overwhelmed her when she saw the white sedan in the ditch on the empty road halfway to the city.

It's not Sam. It can't be Sam.

But the white sedan was none other than Sam's rental car.

He was pinned in the driver's seat. A pool of shattered glass surrounded him. One of his eyes was lacerated and bleeding.

Sydney gulped back nausea. *God, he can't lose his eye.*

The rest of his face and arms were covered with lacerations from the glass and barbed wire. She checked the pulse on his neck.

Weak, but there.

Thank God. He's alive. I have to help him. I have to. Please, Sam, don't die.

Quickly she grabbed her cell phone to call 9-1-1.

No service. *Goddamnit!* She threw the phone into the road. Then, realizing she'd need the phone, she ran into the road and retrieved it.

Thank God it was still working. *Now what? Now what? Now what?*

She had to get help. Had to help Sam.

She touched his bloody cheek. "Sam? Sam, can you hear me?"

His lips twitched.

"It's Sydney, Sam."

More twitching, a soft grunt.

"Can you hear me?"

"Sssss."

Yes! He was trying to reach her. She knew it.

"Sam, listen to me. I'm going to get help. I promise you."

"Sydee," he whispered.

"I'm going to take care of you. I have to leave to get help. My cell phone doesn't have any service. But I will get you to a hospital. I promise. Hold onto that. Please."

"Ssss."

"I love you, Sam O'Donovan, and I promise you, I'm not going to let you die."

She summoned all the strength and courage within her. Leaving him felt all wrong, but she had to.

"I love you," she said again. A tear dropped onto his cheek. Oh no! It probably stung him.

She eased backward, leaving him as still as possible. Then she raced to her car and gunned the engine. She kept going on the route to Denver, checking her cell every thirty seconds for service. When she finally got one bar, she quickly typed in 9-1-1.

Damnit! The call didn't go through.

She tried again.

"9-1-1," the operator said.

"Yes, hello," she said breathlessly. "There's a man on Route 5, about twenty miles outside Bakersville in route to Denver. His car went into a ditch. He's hurt badly. He needs help now!"

"Can you describe the vehicle, ma'am?"

"A white sedan. Might be a Honda. Shit, I don't know. Just get out there!"

"Your name, ma'am?"

"Sydney Buchanan. The man's name is Sam O'Donovan. Please! Now!"

"We'll send an ambulance."

"No! Damnit, not an ambulance. You won't make it in time."

"Ma'am, we need to—"

"The helicopter. Or something better. I'd get him there myself but I can't move him!"

"Ma'am, try to calm down."

"I can't fucking calm down! I love this man! Please help him. God, he can't die. I promised him I wouldn't let him die. Please!"

A few moments elapsed. "Helicopter has been dispatched."

"Thank God. How long?"

"As soon as humanly possible, ma'am. No longer than a half hour."

Damn, too long! But she didn't have a choice. She couldn't do anything else.

She thanked the operator but had a hard time hanging up. The call was her lifeline. Sam's lifeline.

She drove back to Sam. *God, please let him still be alive.*

The sedan shone innocently in the sun, as if it didn't know it held a life in peril. Fear gripped Sydney as she ran toward the car.

Sam sat in the same position she'd left him.

She gulped back her tears. "I'm back, Sam. Help is coming."

No response.

She touched his cheek again. "Sam?"

Still no response.

She took a deep breath and pressed her shaky fingers to his pulse point.

Nothing.

CHAPTER TWENTY-ONE

Oh my God!

"Sam, no! No, no, no!"

This time she couldn't hold back the tears. Why? Why hadn't there been cell service here? Why hadn't she run after him when he left Rena's? Why hadn't she told him about Duke in the first place?

Why?

Why?

Why?

She laid her head in his lap and sobbed. *Please don't leave me, Sam. Please don't leave me.*

She'd promised she wouldn't let him die.

She'd promised.

How would he ever trust her again?

But it didn't matter anymore.

The whipping blades of a helicopter whooshed through the air.

Too late.

Too fucking late.

Sydney didn't move, so lost in Sam she was.

"Get out of the way, ma'am," a voice said.

No. I'm not leaving him.

"Ma'am, move, or I'll move you."

Not leaving him.

Strong hands jerked her from her love.

"No!" she screamed.

Emergency technicians crowded around Sam.

"He's still with us," one said.

Sydney's heart leaped in her chest. Did that mean...?

"Let's get him out of here," another said.

In a few minutes, Sam was on a stretcher with an oxygen mask covering his face.

"Is...is he alive?" she asked.

"Yes, ma'am, but barely." They loaded him on the helicopter.

"Can I come with you? Please?"

"You a relative?"

"Not exactly."

"Then I'm sorry. You can't. We're taking him to Denver General. Meet us there."

Damn! Why hadn't she said yes?

She gunned it all the way to Denver. She had no idea where Denver General was, so she stopped at a convenience store for directions.

And realized she hadn't called Dusty.

She looked at her cell phone. Her fingers had stopped working. How could she call Dusty now? And tell her what? That her parents had taken Duke and Sam had gone half mad? And now he was barely holding onto life and might not make it?

She couldn't formulate the thought herself, let alone tell someone else.

She'd wait. Wait until she got to the hospital and found out how things were. There wasn't anything Dusty could do now anyway.

She found the hospital and went straight to the emergency

room. "Sam O'Donovan?"

The nurse receptionist rustled some papers. "He's in surgery. You a family member?"

"Yes," she said this time. "I'm his fiancée. Sydney Buchanan." *Would that work?* "Can you tell me how he is?"

"I'm sorry, ma'am. I don't know anything. Please have a seat and I'll find you when I have any information."

Sydney sat down in an empty chair. A few chairs down, a young woman held a crying infant. On her other side, an elderly man stared into space. Was he wondering if he should call someone too?

She couldn't put it off any longer. She had to call Dusty.

"Hi, Sydney," Dusty said.

Sydney cleared her throat. "Hi, Dusty. I'm not sure how to tell you this. I'm at Denver General with Sam. He was in a car accident."

"Oh my God! Is he okay?"

"He's in surgery right now. I won't lie to you. It looks pretty bad."

"Oh my God. I'll come right over."

"I don't know how long he'll be in surgery."

"It's okay. I have to be there. He was always there for me."

"Whatever you think is best," Sydney said, though she didn't want company. She wanted to sit alone and pray for Sam.

Sam had to make it.

He had to.

I promise I'll leave him. I won't put him through any more torment. If you spare him, I'll let him go. Clearly I'm not what he needs. I've caused him only pain. But he's innocent in all of this. None of this is his fault. Please let him have his life, and I'll leave. I promise.

Tears fell onto her blouse and she wiped her nose. So she'd live without him. She could do it. It couldn't be that hard to live when your heart was with someone else. She owed it to him. And she'd do it.

The waiting dragged. She leafed through magazine after magazine, not even glancing at the pages.

In an hour, Dusty arrived and gave her a hug. Luckily, after she described what had happened, Dusty wasn't in a talkative mood either. They sat in silence.

And waited.

Sydney lost track of time. Five hours later—six? seven?—a surgeon appeared.

"Miss Buchanan?"

"Yes, that's me." Sydney stood.

"Mr. O'Donovan is in recovery. He's going to make it."

Sydney threw her arms around Dusty. "Oh, thank God! How is he?"

"He had some internal bleeding that we were able to stop. That was the major concern. After that we turned to his eye."

"Oh God," Sydney said.

"Luckily the optic nerve was not severed, but the bleeding was causing quick damage. If we had been even ten minutes later, he would have lost his vision in the right eye."

"Thank God you called when you did, Sydney," Dusty said. "You really came through for him."

Sydney's body froze. She couldn't move, couldn't speak.

"Is there anything else, Doctor?" Dusty asked. "I'm his sister."

"Multiple lacerations on his face and neck, but only a few

of them required stitches. All in all, he was very lucky.

"Thank God," Dusty said.

"Do either of you know what happened? How he ended up in that ditch?"

Dusty shook her head. "Sydney found him."

Sydney tried to speak, but her vocal cords didn't cooperate. She cleared her throat. "I don't know. I found him en route to Denver."

"It's lucky you were on that road when you were," the doctor said.

She nodded. She couldn't speak past the lump in her throat.

"You saved his life."

"Yes, you did," Dusty agreed. "Thank you so much."

Sydney swallowed. She couldn't accept their thanks, their accolades. Their words hung in the air around her, jeering at her.

For the truth of the matter was, had she told Sam the truth about Duke in the first place, he would not have been on that road to Denver, driving to the airport to find her father.

She had been the catalyst for this whole situation. There was no way around it.

It was all her fault.

★ ★ ★

Twenty-four hours later, Sam was moved out of ICU. He was still heavily sedated. After sitting with him for several hours, Sydney realized she had to contact her father and find out what was going on with her mother and with Duke.

Her cell phone had long since died, and she hadn't been

back to her hotel room to charge it. How to get in touch with her father? She could use a hospital phone, of course, but her father's cell phone number had been disconnected. She tried the hotel.

Yes, Mr. Buchanan was registered, but he was not answering at this time. Sydney was bewildered. After all, her parents had prepaid and hadn't bothered checking out, so the clerk on duty could have been referring to their previous reservation. Probably not, though, since security had been notified. Sydney vowed to be optimistic. Roy and Duke had returned to the hotel. They were no doubt wondering where *she* was.

After checking with the reception desk in the waiting area, she found a recharger not in use that fit her phone. Thank goodness. In an hour or so she'd be able to make the calls and find out what was going on.

In the meantime she sat with Sam, holding his hand, hoping her presence soothed him. She couldn't stay with him long-term, but for now, she needed to be with him. Needed to see him through this horrible situation she had caused.

When he was okay again, she would leave.

He was still unresponsive when she left to get her cell phone.

Yes! Two calls had come in from her father. After listening to the voicemails, she learned he had returned to the hotel and he and Duke were in a different room. He left a new cell phone number. Quickly she dialed.

"Sydney," Roy Buchanan said, "where have you been?"

"I'll get to that," she said, "but first, I think it's you who owe me the explanations."

Her father's sigh whooshed into her ear. "Yes, I suppose

you're right about that. Where do I start?"

"How about stealing my purse money and taking Duke away?"

"Your purse money? What are you talking about?"

"Did you or did you not steal my twenty grand out of the safe in my room?"

"Sydney, I didn't. I swear to God."

"Then Mom did."

"How could she...? Oh." His voice clouded. "She did leave for a few minutes before we left the hotel. Did she have access to your room?"

"Of course. I gave her a key."

"Oh no."

"So what's going on? Where is she? You're saying you didn't take my money?

"I did not take your money, Sydney. But why didn't you put it in the safe?"

"I did."

"Then how...? What was your combination?"

"Duke's birthday."

Roy was silent for a moment. Then, "Easy for your mother to guess. She's ill, Sydney. If I wasn't sure before, I sure as hell am now, knowing she stole her daughter's money."

"What happened, Dad? Why did you leave?"

"Your mother was scared that Sam would take us to court and drag Duke through a big mess. I tried to tell her Sam was a nice man, that we'd work something out."

"Sam had decided to talk to you about that, Dad. He also wants what's best for Duke. But honestly, I don't know what he'll do now. There are other circumstances as well. He was—"

"Sydney," Roy interrupted, "please let me explain about

Duke and your mother. I need you to know what's going on. Then you can tell me what's going on at your end."

"All right. Go ahead."

"As I said, your mother was scared about Sam trying to take Duke. She insisted we run. She was adamant. I figured I'd go along with it and head for home. No harm done, right?"

"Well, not exactly."

"Yeah, I know what you mean. After we got on the road, she canceled our cell phones and started to talk about... I don't know how to tell you this."

"Tell me what?"

"About our families, your mother's and mine."

"Don't worry about it. I've talked to Blake. I know everything."

Silence again. Then, "How is your brother?"

"He's had some rough times, but he's doing okay now from what I can tell. He was very willing to help Sam and me find you."

"I'm sure he was. Anyway, if he told you about your mother and me being children of rival crime families in Chicago, he was telling the truth."

"Yes, that's what he told us."

Her father's sigh cut into her ear. "I'm sure you have a lot of questions about that, and I promise I will take the time to tell you everything you want to know, but right now, let me get back to your mother.

"We were taking turns driving. When it was her turn I dozed off for several hours. When I woke up, she had changed our route. She said we were going to Florida to get the money from our Cayman Island account. I assume Blake told you about that?"

"He did."

"Okay. I can only imagine what you must think of us."

"Please, Dad, just go on."

"All these years, I have refused to touch that dirty money. And now, all of a sudden, she wants to get it. She admitted she'd been withdrawing money from the account for years for one reason or another. She also admitted she'd been in contact with her father and taken additional money from him. I was shocked. She knew how I felt about that money.

"She said we were taking Duke out of the country where no one could find us. I told her she was being paranoid, that we'd work it out, but she was determined. Still, I thought she was just stressed out. Until—"

"Until what?"

"She said she was going to call her father and have him take care of Sam."

"Take care of what?"

"That's mob speak. 'Take care of' means have someone killed."

Sydney's heart nearly stopped. "My mother wants to kill Sam?"

"No." Roy cleared his throat. "What I mean is, she's no longer in her right mind."

"Oh my." Sydney didn't know what else to say.

"We were near Branson, so I drove to the nearest hospital and had her committed. After only a few minutes of arguing, she relented. So at least part of her knew it was for the best."

"And you left her in Branson?"

"Not for long. I'm going back. We're going to find the best possible treatment for her. But for now, I need you to take care of Duke. I can't be the single parent to him that he deserves and take care of your mother at the same time. Can you do this for me? For your mother? Can you take care of your son for us?"

Your son. Her father had referred to Duke as *her* son, not his own.

But right now, she had to take care of Sam. "Of course I'll take care of Duke. But I can't take him for a day or two, or maybe more. I have to take care of Sam right now. He's been in a bad car accident."

"What? Oh my God. Is he all right?"

"Yes, he'll be all right." She explained what had happened. "He's lucky he didn't lose the vision in his right eye."

"It sounds like that's because of you."

She sighed. "Maybe. But this whole thing is because of me. If I'd told him about Duke in the first place, none of this would have happened. He and I might be living happily together. Now I can never be with him."

"Why not?"

"Don't you see? I've caused all this. All his pain is because of me."

"But you saved his life."

"If I hadn't kept Duke from him in the first place, he wouldn't have been rushing to the airport to find you. He wouldn't have been in the accident."

"Sydney—" Her father's voice was stern. "This is not your fault. What if I had told your mother 'no' when she wanted to leave? I wanted to, but I didn't. If I had, Sam would also not be in this situation. And neither would you. And neither would Duke. Don't talk to me about guilt. I'm harboring a ton of it. What do you say we both let it go?"

A tear fell from her eye and rolled down her cheek. "I

can't."

"Sydney, you're my daughter and I love you. Please don't let the past dictate the future. We've all made mistakes, but we need to live as things are today. Would I rather your mother not be in the hospital? Of course. But there she will get the help she needs. She is not well, and I'm afraid she hasn't been for some time. I should have seen it.

"Would I rather keep Duke with me? Absolutely. I love that child. He is my son. But I can't give him the life he deserves while I'm trying to take care of his mother. Lucky for me, my daughter, who I know loves him as much as I do, is available to see his life isn't disrupted too much."

"Not disrupted? Don't you think he'll miss you two?"

"Of course he will, but he'll be home with his big sister who adores him and can care for him as well as anyone. He won't be with his distracted father who's trying to do right by him and his mother at the same time."

Sydney sniffed. "I'll just get attached, and when Mom's better, she'll want him back."

"We'll deal with that when the time comes."

"I suppose so. I just—"

"Miss Buchanan?" a nurse interrupted.

"Excuse me, Dad." She turned to the nurse. "Yes?"

"Mr. O'Donovan is awake. He's asking for you."

CHAPTER TWENTY-TWO

"I hear I have you to thank," Sam choked out.

Sydney spoke through tears. "Thank God you're okay. I'm so sorry for all of this, Sam. This is all my fault."

"You promised me you wouldn't let me die."

"You heard that?"

"I heard you. I knew you were there. I wanted to tell you so much, but I couldn't."

"I know. How are you? Are you in much pain?"

"I can't see out of my right eye."

Sydney smiled. "There's a patch on it."

His lips twitched. "Oh."

"But you didn't lose your sight, Sam. You were really lucky."

"Lucky because you got help in time. Like you promised. Thank you."

"Please, don't thank me."

"I—" He choked, and his words came out in a gurgle.

Sydney touched his parched lips with her fingers. "Don't try to talk anymore. Just rest."

"Will you stay?"

"Of course."

Sam dozed off again. Sydney booked a room at a nearby hotel and called her father with the information.

"What have you told Duke about Mom?" she asked.

"Just that she's sick and has to be at the hospital for a while.

He misses her, but he's doing okay. The virus is completely out of his system now and he's eating like a horse."

Sydney smiled. "I'm glad to hear it. Would you...would you consider bringing him to Denver to see Sam? I know it would mean a lot to him."

"Absolutely. There's no reason for us to stay in Bakersville any longer. The rodeo's nearly over."

"Great. You can stay in my room. I have two queen beds."

"We'll be there as soon as we can."

She hung up and called Dusty.

"Should I come up?" Dusty asked.

"No, he's going to be fine. I know you can't miss Harper and Amber's wedding tomorrow."

"I'm sure they would understand."

"Of course they would, but there's no reason for you not to be there. Harper is your sister-in-law's brother. You should be there."

"All right," Dusty relented. "Just take good care of him, okay?"

"Absolutely."

She'd take the best care possible of him.

Before she left.

★ ★ ★

"Well, hello there," Sydney said to Duke. "I've missed you."

"I missed you too, Sassy." The little boy gave her a big hug.

"I hear you and Daddy had quite an adventure."

"Yes. Mama's sick."

"I know. But she'll be better soon."

"And Sam is sick too?"

"Yes, he is. But seeing you will make him feel a lot better."

"Daddy said he had a accident in the car."

"Yes, he was hurt pretty bad. But the doctors fixed him right up."

"Will the doctors fix up Mama too?"

Sydney melted. Duke's big brown eyes shone with love and trust. "Yes, Duke. The doctors will fix Mama." She hoped she wasn't lying to the little boy. "Let's go say hi to Sam, okay?"

A few days had made a big difference in Sam. The lacerations on his face looked much better, though he still wore the eye patch. The doctors said he'd be able to leave in a few more days. He finally felt he looked okay enough to let the little boy visit.

"Look who came to visit," Sydney said, holding Duke's hand as they entered Sam's room.

Sam and Sydney had asked that any machines, other than his IV, be removed before Duke came. The nurses had smiled and said Sam no longer required the other machines, he was doing so well. Now he lay in bed, his lips curved into a smile at the sight of Duke.

"How are you doing, buddy?"

"Fine. I'm sorry you got hurt."

"That's nice of you, but I'm going to be fine."

"Good, I'm glad. My mommy's in the hospital too."

"Yes, I heard. I'm sorry about that, but they're taking really good care of her."

"Yeah, that's what Daddy says."

Sam paused for a moment. "Daddy's right."

Sydney knew immediately the reason for the pause. It was hard for Sam to say "daddy." He thought of himself as Duke's daddy.

They'd agreed Duke wouldn't stay long. They didn't want him to get upset at the sight of Sam.

"We should get going," Sydney said.

"Thanks for coming to see me," Sam said.

"You're welcome. We'll come back soon, won't we, Duke?"

"Sure. We'll come back soon." Duke smiled.

Sydney relinquished Duke into her father's care and went back to Sam.

"Thanks for bringing him," Sam said.

"No need to thank me."

"That's not true. I need to thank you for so many things."

The long fingers of guilt threatened to choke her. "No, you don't."

"Sydney, please. Let me do this."

She sighed and looked around the hospital room. So sterile. So empty. Thank goodness Sam would be leaving soon. He'd have to wear the eye patch for a few weeks, but other than that, he'd get along fine.

"Okay, Sam. Say what you need to say."

"Look at me."

She turned.

His expression glowed with seriousness.

"I love you."

She closed her eyes for a moment. A pang of remorse shot through her. She loved him too, but it didn't matter. She was leaving. She'd made up her mind.

"I love you too."

"Sydney, I'd be dead if it weren't for you."

"I did what anyone would have done."

"You promised you wouldn't let me die, and you didn't.

And you promised you wouldn't leave me here alone, and you didn't."

"Sam, I—"

"Please, let me finish. I love you. Yes, I still wish you'd told me about Duke from the beginning, but I forgive you, Sydney. I forgive you."

Tears welled in her eyes. She didn't deserve his forgiveness. She didn't deserve him.

"And I trust you, Sydney. I trust you with my life."

"Sam, please."

"I want to be a part of your life. I want to be a part of Duke's life. I won't disrupt his life. I'll settle for being his brother-in-law."

Sydney dropped her jaw open. "What?"

"I want to marry you, Sydney." He squeezed her hand. "You are what I've been waiting for all these years. Please. Marry me. You'll make me the happiest man in the world."

Her heart nearly leaped out of her chest. "Sam, are you sure? After all I've done? The lies?"

"I've never been more sure of anything. I love you."

Joy bubbled through her. Could it be true? "Sam, I love you too. I love you so much."

"Then you'll marry me?"

Her mouth trembled as she brushed her lips over his. "Yes, Sam. I'll marry you."

EPILOGUE

"We catched seven Rocky Mountain trouts!" Duke beamed as he held up the fish.

"I catched one and Duke catched two," Sean announced. "Daddy and Uncle Sam catched the rest."

"They're both born fishermen," Zach said. "It's enough for dinner, if you ladies are up to it. The boys can share one, and that leaves one each for you two and two each for Sam and me."

"Ugh, trout?" Sydney rubbed her belly. At ten weeks into her pregnancy, morning sickness—rather, all-day sickness— was at its peak. The thought of putting anything fishy in her mouth made her want to retch.

"Make that two for you then, darlin'," Zach said to Dusty. "Saltines for Sydney, I assume?"

"Sassy eats so many crackers," Duke said. "That's all she eats!"

"You'd rather have crackers than trout?" Sean shook his head.

"Leave Auntie Sydney alone," Dusty said. "When there's a baby inside you, sometimes certain foods make you feel icky."

"Did you feel like that when I was inside you?" Sean asked.

"Goodness yes," Dusty said. "I couldn't eat beef. It darn near killed your daddy that I wouldn't eat his genuine McCray beef."

They all erupted in laughter.

Duke had been living with Sam and Sydney on the

McCray ranch for nearly a year. He missed his parents, but Roy had taken Duke to the hospital twice to visit with Carrie. Sam and Sydney had gone along. Carrie was improving, but it was slow going.

Roy had sold the ranch in Carson City for a decent price and now lived on the McCray ranch as a ranch hand. It was the best way to stay near Duke and be able to see to Carrie's needs. None of them wanted to disrupt the little boy's life.

"Will your mother be able to come home soon?" Dusty asked after the boys had run outside to play.

"Yes, Daddy thinks so. She's chosen to stay longer and get further treatment. She feels terrible about everything and wants to make sure she won't relapse."

"What's going to happen with Duke?"

"We've talked about it. Sam and I are willing to do whatever's best for him. He can stay here with us, or he can move in with Mom and Daddy. Either way, we'll see him often. He's right here on the same ranch."

"Will you ever tell him the truth?"

"Someday, when he's older."

After a dinner of saltines, eaten with a clothespin on her nose to avoid the fish stench, Sydney tucked Duke into bed and joined Sam in their own bedroom.

"I'm beat," Sam said. "A day with those two critters can take it out of a man."

"Hmm, that's too bad." Sydney smiled. "Those crackers settled my tummy, and now I'm feeling"—she reached over for his erection—"a little frisky."

"Oh yeah?" He rolled toward her. "I think I can accommodate you."

Sydney turned, reached into her nightstand drawer, and

pulled out two bandanas.

Sam's eyebrows shot up. "I didn't think you wanted to try that again."

She winked at him. "That's what you get for thinking."

CONTINUE THE TEMPTATION SAGA WITH BOOK SEVEN

Tantalizing
MARIA

Available Now

MESSAGE FROM HELEN HARDT

Dear Reader,

Thank you for reading *Trusting Sydney*. If you want to find out about my current backlist and future releases, please like my Facebook page: **www.facebook.com/HelenHardt** and join my mailing list: **www.helenhardt.com/signup/**. I often do giveaways. If you're a fan and would like to join my street team to help spread the word about my books, you can do so here: **www.facebook.com/groups/hardtandsoul/**. I regularly do awesome giveaways for my street team members.

If you enjoyed the story, please take the time to leave a review on a site like Amazon or Goodreads. I welcome all feedback.

I wish you all the best!

Helen

ALSO BY HELEN HARDT

The Sex and the Season Series:
Lily and the Duke
Rose in Bloom
Lady Alexandra's Lover
Sophie's Voice
The Perils of Patricia (Coming Soon)

The Temptation Saga:
Tempting Dusty
Teasing Annie
Taking Catie
Taming Angelina
Treasuring Amber
Trusting Sydney
Tantalizing Maria

The Steel Brothers Saga:
Craving
Obsession
Possession
Melt (Coming December 20th, 2016)
Burn (Coming February 14th, 2017)
Surrender (Coming May 16th, 2017)

Daughters of the Prairie:
The Outlaw's Angel
Lessons of the Heart
Song of the Raven

ACKNOWLEDGMENTS

Like the first book in the *Temptation Saga, Tempting Dusty, Trusting Sydney's* main characters are named after former dogs of mine, Sam and Sydney. I hope you enjoyed the story of two people learning to trust each other against the odds.

So many people helped along the way in bringing this book to you. Celina Summers, Michele Hamner Moore, Jenny Rarden, Cera Smith, Kelly Shorten, David Grishman, Meredith Wild, Jonathan Mac, Kurt Vachon, Yvonne Ellis, Shayla Fereshetian—thank you all for your expertise and guidance. Eternal thanks to Waterhouse Press for the expert rebranding of the series.

And thanks most of all to you, the readers. Who else would like to read about in the *Temptation Saga?* A book is coming...and I'll leave you to guess whose story it will be.

ABOUT THE AUTHOR

New York Times and *USA Today* Bestselling author Helen Hardt's passion for the written word began with the books her mother read to her at bedtime. She wrote her first story at age six and hasn't stopped since. In addition to being an award winning author of contemporary and historical romance and erotica, she's a mother, a black belt in Taekwondo, a grammar geek, an appreciator of fine red wine, and a lover of Ben and Jerry's ice cream. She writes from her home in Colorado, where she lives with her family. Helen loves to hear from readers.

Visit her here:
www.facebook.com/HelenHardt

After being left at the altar, Jade Roberts seeks solace at her best friend's ranch on the Colorado western slope. Her humiliation still ripe, she doesn't expect to be attracted to her friend's reticent brother, but when the gorgeous cowboy kisses her, all bets are off.

Talon Steel is broken. Having never fully healed from a horrific childhood trauma, he simply exists, taking from women what is offered and giving nothing in return...until Jade Roberts catapults into his life. She is beautiful, sweet, and giving, and his desire for her becomes a craving he fears he'll never be able to satisfy.

Passion sizzles between the two lovers...but long-buried secrets haunt them both and may eventually tear them apart.

Visit HelenHardt.com for more information!